P9-CJC-881

FATAL FASCINATOR

Jenn McKinlay

BERKLEY PRIME CRIME
New York

BERKLEY PRIME CRIME
Published by Berkley
An imprint of Penguin Random House LLC
penguinrandomhouse.com

ISBN: 9780593546772

First Edition: January 2023

Printed in the United States of America
1 3 5 7 9 10 8 6 4 2

Book design by Laura K. Corless

For Jan Buckwalter, one of the best people I know.
I'm proud to call you my friend. Thanks for always
helping me with the critters both domestic and wild.

Chapter 1

"Bella, sit. Sit, Bella." She didn't sit. "Want a treat? I'll give you a treat if you sit or just aim your bottom in the general direction of the ground." I swear she smiled at me as if this had been her ploy all along.

Bella was the corgi puppy that my fiancé, Harrison Wentworth, and I had adopted several months ago in a case of cute-puppy-induced delirium. She wiggled her heart-shaped bottom and cocked her head to the side. I was undone by the adorableness and tossed the treat in the air. She nabbed it before it completed its arc.

"Scarlett Parker, did you just give that dog a treat when she didn't even do what you asked?"

I turned and saw my friend and neighbor Andre Eisel strolling down Portobello Road toward me while shaking his head. A strikingly handsome man with diamond ear studs that winked at me in the morning light, he was wearing jeans, a white T-shirt that showed off his dark complexion, beneath a black blazer with the collar turned up, and thickly soled combat boots. He was a professional photographer, and his impeccable sense of style was enough to make me feel dowdy in my brown ankle boots, cream-colored midi dress and loose-fitting navy cardigan.

Bella recognized him immediately and simply lost her puppy mind, barking and jumping as if she never received any attention at all. Honestly, from her behavior, a person would think I habitually left her outside in the cold, chained to the gate. The little conniver.

"Bella, my love," Andre cried. He immediately dropped into a squat and gave her all the affection her doggy heart could hold.

"Encouraging her histrionics is not helpful," I said.

He glanced up at me, completely unrepentant. "Where's Harrison?"

"He had to go into the office early today," I said. "So, I'm bringing Bella to Mim's Whims with me."

"Viv is going to love that," Andre said, eyebrows raised.

"Meh, she'll get over it," I said. "She won't admit it, but she secretly loves Bella."

Andre rose to his feet and fell into step beside me. It was a glorious May morning. The sun was warm, the air was cool, the birds were— Bella stopped our walk to do her business. Again.

"Here." I handed Andre the leash. He made a face

2

while I took out a biodegradable bag and cleaned up after my girl. I tossed it into a nearby bin, and she glanced at me over her shoulder with her little tongue hanging out of her mouth. "Who's Mama's good girl?"

She wiggled and I gave her another treat, bending over to pat her soft head.

"She's going to get fat," Andre observed. He squatted down beside me and pointed to Bella's round tummy.

"Hush," I said. I clapped my hands over her ears. "She'll hear you and you'll scar her for life."

"I would never—"

"Andre! Yoo-hoo!" Andre glanced across the street, where a tall, curvy brunette stood waving. She was dressed head to toe in designer clothes, from her pink Christian Louboutin heels, to her blue silk Stella McCartney dress, to her matching pink Chanel bag.

"*Ack!* Hide me," Andre said. I glanced at his face. He wasn't joking.

"Who is she?"

"*Bridus horribilis,*" he muttered. "Piper May, about as posh as they come. Her wedding is next month. I've been dodging her for weeks."

"But you're a photographer," I said. "Aren't wedding gigs your bread and butter while you pursue your artsy photos on the side?"

"They are, but her wedding is in the country and I hate the country." He shuddered, emphasizing his point. Bella took this as an invitation to offer comfort, and she hopped up and licked his chin. "Also, I loathe her fiancé."

"That is problematic," I agreed.

"Do you think if I pretend not to see her, she'll go away?" he asked.

I glanced over his shoulder. Piper May was on the move, jogging on her tiptoes and dodging pedestrians, bicycles, and moms with strollers . . . er . . . prams, as the locals say, to get to Andre.

"Not a chance," I said. "That is a woman on a mission, and if you try to escape, she'll run you to the ground."

"Blast!" Andre muttered beneath his breath.

We rose to our feet, resigning ourselves to the unavoidable meeting.

"Piper, how are you?" Andre greeted the woman as she hopped up onto the sidewalk. They air-kissed each other's cheeks, and then she stepped back and narrowed her eyes.

"You've been avoiding me," she accused. She had a long waterfall of dark brown hair, and thick eyebrows that had been shaped into arched accent marks that highlighted her big brown eyes, high cheekbones and dainty chin. She was a very attractive woman, but I wondered how much of it was dependent upon the thick coating of makeup she wore.

"I would never," Andre declared in a flagrant fib. "Nick and I have just been so busy with his vineyard in France, I haven't had a minute to myself."

This was true. Nick Carroll, Andre's life partner, had recently invested in a friend's vineyard in Provence and when he wasn't busy with his dental practice, Nick was off tending his vines, taking Andre with him. Nick had big dreams of retiring to the South of France to pursue a second career as a vintner. Andre was dubious but kept his reservations to himself and to me. Lucky me.

"Piper May, this is my friend and neighbor Scarlett Parker, one of the proprietors of Mim's Whims."

"Hi—" I began but Piper interrupted.

"Mim's Whims?" she cried. "Then you know Vivian Tremont."

"She's my cousin," I confirmed. "We inherited the shop from our grandmother Mim."

"That's right," she said. She looked me over from head to foot in an assessing glance, as if trying to place me on the social food chain. "You're the American who bagged Harrison Wentworth." Before I could confirm, she wagged a pointy acrylic nail at me and continued, "The one who went viral as the 'party crasher.'"

I sighed. It seemed that neither time nor distance would allow me to leave my sordid past in the past. I mean, you have one bad day when you stumble upon the anniversary party that your boyfriend, whom you thought was single, is throwing for his wife, you inadvertently throw some cake at him, and *BAM!*—you're labeled the party crasher for life. It wasn't fair. I blamed my red hair. If I were a cool brunette like the woman standing before me, I was quite certain the video would not have gotten the 3.2 million views it had.

"Yes, that's me," I said. At least the part about bagging Harrison Wentworth seemed to be a compliment, although I would argue that it was him who bagged me.

"Well, you are just the person I need," Piper said. She slid her arm through mine as if we were old friends—

pushy!—and then began to walk in the direction of the shop, leaving Andre and Bella to follow.

I noted that Bella did not jump on Piper. In fact, it appeared to me that she was giving her side-eye as if jealous that Piper had managed to draw the attention of the adults away from her canine self. I could sympathize. No one likes a limelight thief.

"With what do you need help?" I asked.

"My wedding," Piper said. "Specifically, the fascinators for the bridal party."

"Isn't your wedding next month?" I asked.

"Yes," she said. Her long legs ate up the sidewalk with determined efficiency. I had to scurry to keep up. Andre was behind us, looking relieved that I was the one who was presently the focus of Piper's attention. "I'm in a fizz, as my original designer, Javier Sebastian, has been embroiled in a scandal."

"Scandal?" Andre chimed in from behind us.

Piper waved her free hand dismissively. "He murdered his lover by putting cyanide in his food and then fled the country with my money all because of his little drama. I need to get this sorted right away."

"Little drama," I repeated.

I glanced over my shoulder at Andre to see if he was getting this. He raised his eyebrows and made a face that told me he was equally horrified and, yet, not surprised.

"Where did he even get cyanide?" I asked. "I mean, it's not like you can just pick it up at the Tesco in the how-to-lose-a-lover section."

Piper turned her head to look at me. She examined me

from head to toe again, and I was immediately as self-conscious as a middle-schooler with a pimple on the end of their nose.

"You're funny," she said. But she didn't laugh. "Vivian probably enjoys that." She didn't say it, but I felt it was implied that she did not—enjoy it, that is.

"I read an article recently that poison is easily purchased off the Internet," Andre said. "We're living in very scary times."

"Indeed," Piper agreed. "Which is why I need Viv to save my wedding."

"About Viv," I said. "She usually requires months to create custom designs for weddings, so I'm not sure she'll be able to—"

"Nonsense," Piper said. "With all of the royals married off, mine is the wedding of the year. Viv will want her stamp all over it."

"Viv?" I repeated. I glanced at the determined set to Piper's jaw, which was level with my eyes. "It sounds as if you two know each other."

"Viv and I go way back," she confirmed. She didn't elaborate, but given that Viv had never mentioned Piper to me, I assumed they were acquaintances from university. Viv and I had been less close during those years.

"So, you're friends?" I asked. I felt the need to understand what I was getting into before we stepped into the hat shop.

"Not precisely," Piper said. She kept her gaze forward as the shop came into view.

The blue-and-white-striped awning was out, and the

sign on the inside of the door was flipped to *Open*. This had to be because Fiona "Fee" Felton, Viv's assistant, had arrived early today. Viv never bothered to unlock the doors or flip the sign.

I suspected if Fee or I didn't show up, Viv would keep the awning tucked in and the door locked all day. Viv was not what I would call a people person, which was primarily why I was feeling nervous about walking into the shop arm in arm with Piper. If Viv didn't like her, the potential for a scene was high.

"Are you enemies then?" I persisted. I tried to pull my arm out of her grip but she tightened her fingers, not allowing my escape.

"Not exactly," she said. She paused in front of the door and turned to face me, releasing my arm. Thank goodness. She looked thoughtful and said, "Frenemies. Viv and I are definitely what I would call frenemies."

This did not sit well with me at all. Viv didn't have frenemies. She had friends or enemies. There was no gray area in between and definitely no mash-ups.

Before I could think to move, Piper grasped the door handle and yanked it open. She strode inside as if she owned the place, and I felt Andre step up behind me.

"Now you see why I was avoiding her," he muttered. "The woman is a force."

I glanced over my shoulder at him and lifted my right eyebrow. "So is Viv. This could get ugly."

"Do you think there will be actual bloodshed?" he asked.

"Doubtful," I said. "Probably just a delicious setdown. Viv isn't the violent sort."

"I do love a tasty battle of wits." He grinned.

Together we entered the shop, anticipating the drama that was about to unfold. We were woefully disappointed.

"Vivian!" Piper called. She raised her arm and gave a little finger wave.

Viv was standing on the opposite side of the shop. She was fussing with a series of mannequin heads all sporting her latest creations. Viv had been on an organza bender last month, crafting luscious, frothy confections in brilliant shades of yellow and orange, magenta and purple. It had felt like having yards and yards of a sunset swallowing up the shop, which was rather delightful, actually.

Viv turned slowly to face us. Her long blond curls reached halfway down her back, and she was wearing a formfitting blue dress that perfectly matched her large eyes. Our eyes were the only feature we shared, inherited from Mim. Viv was all creamy skin and wicked curves, while I was pale, freckles and stick-straight red hair with a figure to match. Honestly, if I didn't love her like a sister, I'd be consumed with jealousy. When Viv was in a room, everyone stopped and stared, and I do mean everyone. Except Piper, apparently.

"How are you, darling?" Piper strode across the room with her arms held wide.

Bella sat down, planting her rump on my toes. Her head cocked to the side as if she, too, could not comprehend the audacity of this person who thought she could cold-call Vivian Tremont—acclaimed milliner, mild eccentric and temperamental artist—and live to tell about it.

To my shock, Viv smiled a real, genuine, teeth-showing grin and cried, "Piper!"

As if this weren't stunning enough, the two women hugged. Hugged! Well, technically, I suppose it was an air hug. They didn't actually touch each other but sort of leaned into each other's proximity and made kissing noises in the vicinity of each other's faces.

"I'm gobsmacked," Andre said.

"Ditto," I agreed. It felt as if the planet had shifted on its axis without warning. "Viv looks genuinely happy to see her."

"And Viv is never happy to see anyone," he said.

"It's alarming," I concluded.

"What brings you by, Piper?" Viv asked. She looked her friend over, clearly approving of her cheerful spring ensemble. I knew Viv well enough to know that she was already debating which hat would best complement Piper's outfit.

"Betrayal," Piper said. She dragged out the word for full dramatic effect.

Andre and I didn't even pretend not to be listening. Piper was building her case for Viv to step in and save her wedding. I couldn't help but wonder if it would work.

"Do tell," Viv said. She gestured to the deep blue love seat and two matching armchairs arranged in the corner of the shop in front of an old wardrobe of my grandmother's. I glanced at the antique cabinet that sported a large carved bird on the top with its wings spread out. I had dubbed him Ferd the bird when I moved in several years ago, and while I supposed it sounded overly imaginative, I truly thought he listened to everything that was said in the shop.

Piper dropped her purse at her feet and sank down onto one of the armchairs as if she were about to collapse. She was full-on damsel in distress. Then she heaved a sigh that sounded as if it had come all the way up from her feet.

Bella, of course, took this as an invitation to join Piper in her chair. Only Andre's quick reflexes managed to snatch her out of the air before the pup's diving leap landed her in Piper's lap. Andre met my gaze over the head of the wiggling puppy with a look that told me I owed him one, and then turned to the others and said, "Shall I fix some tea?"

"That would be lovely, Andre, thank you," Piper said.

Viv pursed her lips as if she wasn't pleased with Piper making herself quite so at home. I wandered over to the main counter in the shop and started to busy myself with rearranging a pile of invoices for materials. It felt much like pushing my broccoli around on my plate as a kid and trying to convince my parents it was actually getting eaten when it was really just doing laps. Neither Viv nor Piper paid any attention to me, so I assumed it was working.

"Tell me what's happened," Viv said.

"Javier Sebastian happened. He fled the country with the money I paid him to make my bridesmaids' fascinators," Piper said.

"Oh, dear, that's awful," Viv said. She settled into the love seat, propping her elbow on the armrest and her chin in her hand as she considered Piper's tale of woe. "I thought Javier was the most sought-after hat designer in town, no?"

I was quite certain I was not imagining the note of satisfaction in Viv's voice, and suddenly her gracious welcome of Piper made perfect sense. She knew. She knew Javier had split town. She knew Piper was in a jam. And she was enjoying every bit of the grovel show. Huh.

"Just to be perfectly clear, *I* didn't want to hire him," Piper said. "My mother insisted. We met him at India Couture Week last year and he was all the rage. You know how my mother is, so concerned about what everyone will think all the time. Javier was the flavor of the month after he designed Hannah Waddingham's iconic hat in the last season of *Ted Lasso*. There was simply no talking her out of him."

"The cost of life in the society pages, I suppose," Viv said. She made a sympathetic noise in the back of her throat. She didn't have me fooled one little bit, however.

"You know you're my absolute favorite milliner in the whole wide world," Piper gushed. I thought she might be putting it on a little thick there but Viv didn't seem to mind.

"Thank you," Viv said. "I imagine the loss of the bridesmaids' hats is quite a crushing blow."

"I'll say," Piper said. "They cost seven hundred pounds each, and I have seven bridesmaids. My father about had a fit. He's horribly tight and has been such a scrooge about the entire wedding."

Viv nodded. She was used to the expense of custom-designed millinery, but I was not. Being an American, I didn't entirely grasp the whole hat thing. Even though I'd grown up in Mim's Whims during my school holidays and summer breaks, and I appreciated the artistry that went into each one, I was still frequently caught off guard by how much a single hat could cost.

"Such a shame," Viv said. "Perhaps you can find something suitable at Harrods?"

Piper made a pained face. "Off the rack? Really, Viv, there's no need to be cruel."

A small smile curved Viv's lips. Whatever she'd been about to say was interrupted by Andre with a tea tray. Bella was not with him, so I assumed he'd left her with Fee in the workroom. I knew I should probably go and check on my baby but I wanted to know what was going to happen between Viv and Piper. I watched from my spot at the counter while Andre served them.

"Cuppa, Scarlett?" he asked me.

"Yes, please," I said. This was all the invitation I needed to join the ladies. I took the seat next to Viv on the love seat, leaving the other armchair for Andre.

He handed me a delicate china cup of tea, prepared with milk and sugar exactly as I liked it, which was a true mark of friendship in my book. I took a cautious sip. Perfection.

"Viv." Piper paused to sip her tea. She beamed her thanks at Andre. "Are you really going to make me beg?"

"Of course not," Viv said. "I would never be so hateful, especially since there is no amount of begging that could change the circumstance."

13

"The circumstance?" Piper repeated. "I'm sorry. I don't think I'm following."

"The simple fact is that while I know you're hoping that I can help your situation, I just don't have enough time to design and produce hats for your wedding, which is in, what, six weeks?"

"Eight weeks, at the end of June. But, Viv, you have to," Piper wailed. "My wedding will be ruined without you, absolutely ruined."

I glanced at Andre. He ignored me and blew delicately on the tea in his cup. Obviously, Piper's dramatics were nothing new to him.

"Dearest, so long as you and the groom show up, I sincerely doubt your wedding could be ruined by your bridesmaids' hats, or lack thereof," Viv said.

"Oh, it'll be ruined. Whatever would people say? My mother would have an absolute episode. No, it's completely unacceptable to have a hatless bridal party. I mean, we're not savages," Piper said. She glanced at me and said, "No offense."

I sipped my tea and shot my pinkie out as if that proved I wasn't a barbarian from America.

"Viv, I'll do anything," Piper wheedled. "You know, with all of the royals now married off, my wedding is to be the wedding of the year. I can't have some second-rate milliner for the bridal party. It has to be you."

"I'm sure you'll find some resourceful up-and-coming milliner willing to fill the void," Viv said. She set her cup on its saucer and placed it on the low table in front of us, indicating that the discussion was over. She looked every inch the picture of millinery royalty that she was.

Piper's face became pinched, and she looked like she was considering having a tantrum. Her face cleared as she thought better of it. Good call. Tantrums never worked on Viv, they just got customers banned for life.

"How about this: Why don't you come to the wedding as our guest of honor?" Piper asked. "You could stay the entire weekend. We're getting married at Waverly Castle in Sussex, you know. Lots of hills, fields, sheep and quaint little villages. You could use it as a holiday."

I saw Andre shudder. I wondered if it was the hills, fields, or sheep that he objected to.

"Andre is our photographer and he'll be there all weekend," Piper said.

"Right. Wait . . . what? Me? I'm your photographer?" Andre asked.

Piper turned her enormous brown eyes on him and blinked once, then twice, and then added a lip tremble. Andre was a goner. I'd known him for years now and he was useless with tears, anyone's tears—child, woman, man, didn't matter. Tears hit him like a wrecking ball.

"Yes, of course. Do not tell me you're backing out, too. I mean, you promised me, Andre," Piper said.

"I did?" He looked alarmed that he might have made a promise of which he had no recall.

"Yes," she said. "When you took our engagement photos, I asked you to do the wedding and you said yes."

Andre frowned. "I did? I don't remember. That was a rather stressful day."

"I know Dooney was late and not behaving his best," Piper said. "But you know he'll show up for the wedding and he'll have his company manners, I promise."

"I—" Andre began but she interrupted him.

"I'm counting on you, Andre." She said it with the firmness of a governess disciplining a student. Andre wasn't having it.

"When we took your engagement photos, Piper, I was under the impression that the wedding would be in town," he said. "I only heard that it was in the country from another client."

"Perhaps it was, that was months ago after all." Piper nodded thoughtfully. "No matter. I've always dreamed of being married in a castle, and Waverly is stunning. My father managed to convince them to rent the entire place to us for the big day. It's going to be the grandest wedding since Will and Kate. The main staircase is the stuff of fairy tales. You're going to love taking pictures of me when I make my grand entrance."

"It sounds amazing," I said. I wondered if this was something Harry and I should consider, a big old castle to tie the knot in.

Harrison was an investment wizard in the financial district, and I knew if I really wanted a castle for our ceremony, he'd be game, but was a castle really who we were? Then again, he had a new business with a lot of people to impress, so maybe it was. Hmm.

"You should come, too, Scarlett," Piper said. I turned

to look at her. It was like she could read my mind. "After all, Waverly Castle is the hottest spot for a society wedding, and this would give you a chance to check it out while it's in use."

"That's a brilliant idea," I said.

"No." Viv smashed my hopes to bits without even a smidgeon of remorse. "We have too much happening in town. Ascot is in mid-June and it's one of our biggest events of the year. We have so much to do before then, we simply can't take on another wedding. I really am sorry, Piper."

Her voice was full of regret, and I thought it was actually genuine.

"But my wedding is two weeks after Ascot," Piper protested. "You will absolutely need a rest after that and the castle has a spa."

"A spa," I said. Visions of massages, facials and mud baths danced in my head.

I glanced at Viv. She was the artist and I wouldn't push but, oh, getting away for a weekend after the flurry of Ascot would be fabulous timing.

"Having the wedding after Ascot does change things a smidge," Viv said.

"We can go together," Andre said. "It'll be fun."

He didn't sound like he thought it would be fun. He sounded like he was trying to convince us that dancing on hot coals was a great idea.

"I think Fee can handle the shop for a couple of days," I said.

"And what about Bella?" Viv asked. "Are you just going to abandon your baby at the first chance you get to go play in a castle?"

"No," I said. *Yes.* "She'll be with Harry, and she can go visit Aunt Betty and Freddy, who'll be delighted to have her."

"That's true," Andre said. "Aunt Betty dotes on Bella, as does Freddy."

I turned and glanced at Andre. He had a look of desperation in his dark brown eyes that shouted louder than words that he absolutely didn't want to have to go out to the country by himself.

"Who is Aunt Betty?" Piper asked. Then she tipped her head to the side. "Never mind, I don't care. No dogs at the wedding. Dooney is allergic."

"Of course he is," Andre muttered.

I shot him a questioning glance, which he ignored.

Aunt Betty was Harrison's aunt. She had entered her Freddy, also a corgi, in a dog show last year. In a roundabout way, that was the entire reason Harry and I had adopted Bella, whom I loved as if she were my firstborn. But even new mamas needed a break every now and again, and a spa in a castle sounded like just the ticket.

"Oh, come on, Viv, we can do it," I said. "A castle. Just think how cool that will be. Plus, it's the wedding of the year. We don't want to miss out on that publicity."

Viv couldn't care less if it was the wedding of the year. She was an artist first and a businessperson second, whereas I was a people person first and not a businessperson at all. This was why we needed Harrison so much, to help keep the money side of things in the black.

Viv pursed her lips, considering.

"And Andre will be there," I said. "The three of us can soak up the inspiration of a nice English spring and sip boba tea while wrapped in seaweed."

Viv frowned. She enjoyed the country about as much as Andre did. Neither one of them were completely comfortable unless there was a Tube stop within walking distance.

"Isn't there a famous hatmaker in East Sussex?" Andre asked. "Dominick Falco, does that name sound familiar?"

"Sound familiar?" Viv cried. "He's one of the best milliners in England. His designs were revolutionary in the seventies. When his wife died, he packed up his studio and left London. No one knew where he went, and he doesn't design professionally anymore. I'd heard he was a recluse but I had no idea he lived in the country. I thought he'd taken off for France or Italy."

"Nope." Andre glanced up from his phone. "It says here that he lives in the village near Waverly Castle."

Andre met my gaze and winked. Well, color me impressed. How had he thought to look for hat designers in Sussex to leverage Viv into going? Brilliant!

"We have to visit him," I said. I sensed Viv's resistance was crumbling. We just needed to hammer it in the right spot. "I'm betting he'd be thrilled to talk shop with another milliner after so many years in seclusion."

Viv bit her lip as she considered. She glanced up at Piper. "With this little time, the hats won't be ready until the wedding, and quite possibly the very day of the wedding. You're going to have to pay a rush fee and I will have complete artistic control. What I design is what you get, no quibbling."

"Understood." Piper sat up straight. "I'm sure I'll adore whatever you create."

"Of course you will," Viv said. She sounded bored. She reached across the table and took Piper's cup out of her hands and set it down on the tray. She then gathered the rest of our cups. She lifted the tray and headed for the workroom. "Work out the details with Scarlett. I need to think."

"Don't you want to know the color and style of my bridesmaids' dresses?" Piper asked. Her eyes went wide in alarm.

"Not necessary," Viv said. She carried the tray on one hand and waved her other hand dismissively.

"Oh, goodness, what have I done?" Piper asked. I was certain she had visions of hats that clashed with her chosen colors or were an artistic statement of Viv's that would overshadow her, the bride, on her special day.

"You're not the first bride to ask that question," Andre said.

I shot him a quelling look. This was actually why I was needed at the hat shop. I was the customer pleaser, the client liaison, the person who convinced the patron that wearing an enormous peacock on her head really was the height of fashion. Thankfully, I'd only had to do that once. A photo of the woman had made the society pages above the fold, and she was delighted with the notoriety.

"What colors have you chosen?" I asked Piper.

"Blush," she said. "Silk with high waists, mini length, and cap sleeves."

"Sounds lovely." I nodded, stifling a yawn.

This had been the chosen color for every bride we'd designed hats for all season. I had no doubt that Viv had walked away without asking because she knew exactly what color she was going to be dealing with. She was fashion savvy like that.

"I'll let Viv and Fee know," I said. "I am positive she will create something amazing."

Piper rose to her feet. Satisfaction curved her lips in a triumphant smile. "I'm sure she will."

She strode across the room to the door, where she paused and said, "I'll be in touch."

"Cheers," Andre said through gritted teeth.

"Looking forward to it," I called and waved until the door shut after her. Then I turned to Andre and hugged him. "This is going to be so great. A castle, Andre! An actual castle."

He glanced down at me. He wasn't smiling. "There are probably spiders and rats and an angry ghost residing in the old pile of stones."

"A ghost?" I asked. "Really?"

"Scarlett, this is England, you know every place has a ghost," he said. "It's like a point of pride."

I thought about the scent of lily of the valley that occasionally appeared in the shop. Both Viv and I had come across it at various times, and it was a scent we associated with Mim, as it had been her signature perfume when she was alive. Did I think she was still here in the hat shop? Maybe.

"So what if there's a ghost?" I asked. I was trying to

cheer him up. "You'll have me and Viv to scare away any mean spirits, squash any spiders or catch any rats." That was a lie. I wasn't catching any rats or squashing any spiders, but Andre didn't need to know that. "It's going to be a wonderful adventure. You'll see."

He didn't look like he believed me. Not one little bit.

Chapter 2

"Ginger, how much luggage could you possibly need for a weekend?" Harry asked. He was trying to wedge my third suitcase into the boot of his car. It wasn't cooperating.

I gazed at my handsome fiancé with his tousled, wavy brown hair, piercing green eyes, and ruddy cheeks and felt myself get just a little dizzy. Harry was the only person who called me Ginger, because of my hair, and even though he'd done it to annoy me when we first met as kids, now it made me smile.

Harry—I was the only person who called him that for the same reason—let out an exasperated huff, and I sidled up next to him and gazed at him from beneath my lashes in what I hoped was my steamy come-hither look. It tended to make him lose his concentration or at least distract him from whatever I'd done to peeve him. His nostrils flared and I batted my eyelashes.

"Flirting with me will not distract me from the situation at hand, love, which is that you have too much luggage," he said. Then he leaned down and kissed me quick as if to let me know that he wasn't annoyed, or at least not super annoyed. "You're going to have to make some choices."

"But I've never been to the countryside," I protested. "How will I know what to wear if I don't pack a lot of options?"

"Wellies," a voice said from behind me. "You need wellies and a wool jumper to keep the mud and the chill away."

"Nick!" I whirled around, stepped forward and hugged him tight.

Nick Carroll was a dentist by trade but in our little squad of friends, he was mostly known for being a snappy dresser. Today he was in a lavender-and-purple-striped dress shirt with the cuffs rolled back to reveal a paisley print. His trousers were beige linen and his loafers a soft buttery leather in a dark shade of brown. He wore a panama hat on his thinning strawberry blond hair and looked every inch the vintner he was learning to be.

"Are you here to see us off?" I asked.

"Of course," he said. "Although Andre made me check him for a fever three times this morning. I think he was hoping he contracted the flu so he could get out of going. He really hates the country."

24

"You don't say," I said, my tone as dry as melba toast. Andre had been complaining for the past eight weeks about Piper May's wedding at Waverly Castle.

Nick laughed. He shook hands with Harry and said, "Need a hand, mate?"

"More like a bigger boot," Harry said. He pulled everything out of the trunk of the car for the third time and began to rearrange it all again.

"Oh, you'll manage," I said. "You always do." I batted my lashes again, and he sighed and turned back to the car. The man was a master at *Tetris*; surely he could figure this out.

"And where are you off to while we waste away in the countryside?" I asked Nick. "Back to France to tend your vines?"

"Sadly, no," he said. "I have to perform an emergency root canal on Mrs. Delancy. She's called the office six times. I can't in good conscience leave her in pain. Plus, Andre would be put out with me if I took off to France without him."

"Your vineyard is in the countryside in Provence," I said. "Why doesn't Andre mind going there but he balks at Sussex?"

"Because it's France, pet," Nick said. "Besides, I keep him drunk most of the time so he's too soused to notice any terrifying wildlife."

"Tricky, very tricky," I said. "I'll keep that in mind in case we see a rat in the castle."

"There's a rat in the castle?" Andre squeaked as he walked up behind Nick.

"No, no," I said. I didn't want Andre to panic and cancel. Piper would freak out, and then I'd have to deal with Viv on my own. I loved my cousin like a sister, truly, but she could be a handful. "Cat, I said cat."

"I don't like cats either," Andre said.

"Liar," Nick said. "Who's the one who has been lobbying for a cat, and a long-haired one at that? You. You're just looking for an excuse to get out of this wedding and it's not just because you hate the country. Now let's get this sorted once and for all. Why don't you want to photograph Piper May's wedding?"

"No reason," Andre said. He turned his close-shaven head away, giving us an excellent view of his profile. It was a good one, with a strong chin and a long nose.

"No one believes you," Nick said. He turned to me. "Back me up, Scarlett."

"You do seem more resistant than is warranted for a weekend *in a castle*," I said. I emphasized what I considered to be the high point.

"All right, fine," Andre said. He gently lowered his shoulder bag with all of his equipment to the ground. "I have a history with the groom, Dooney Portis."

My eyes went wide. "When you say history . . ."

"No, not like that. We weren't involved or anything," Andre said. He shuddered and made a gagging face. "Heaven forbid."

"Well, that's a relief," Nick said. "Talk about awkward. No bride wants the man photographing her new husband to know him as well as she does."

"Oh, it's still awkward," Andre assured him. "He used to torture me in grade school."

I frowned. "I hate him already."

"Agreed," Harry said. He paused in packing the trunk—excuse me, boot—to join the conversation. "I take it he was a bully?"

"Yes, the worst," Andre said. "He was consumed with being the most popular kid in school, and heaven help anyone who he thought might take the light off him."

"Which you did," I said. "Because you're charming and handsome and brilliant."

Andre shrugged. "I was well-liked, let's leave it at that. It didn't sit well with Dooney, and he followed me home from school every day threatening to hurt me if I didn't stop being popular. Like how does a person do that? There's not some switch you can flip to fade back into obscurity."

"What kind of name is Dooney anyway?" Nick asked. "How did he expect to be popular with a moniker like that? It makes him sound like a biscuit."

I laughed. Nick was right. "Biscuit" was the British word for "cookie," and Dooney certainly sounded like Jaffa Cake or Jammie Dodger. And suddenly, I was hankering for a biscuit.

"It is a crumby name," Harry quipped.

"Half-baked for certain," Andre joined in.

We all laughed. Our little group did love their puns.

"Dough not get me started," Nick said.

"Bake-ause you'd never quit," I joked.

They all turned to look at me with pitying expressions, except for Harry, who grinned. He was the only one who appreciated my puns, but I think it was only because we were engaged and he was required to.

"Oh, come on," I said. "Bake-cause, funny, right?"

Andre and Nick just shook their heads.

"I picked up some snacks for the trip, yeah," Fee said as she stepped out of the hat shop carrying a Marks & Spencer bag.

"Are there any biscuits in there?" I asked as she handed it to me.

"Of course," she said. "You can't go on a road trip without some digestives."

I had learned these were actually much tastier than the name suggests.

"Excellent," I said and she beamed. "Thank you."

Fee was tall and lithe with dark skin and eyes. Her face was heart shaped with a pointy chin, and she wore her cork-screw curls in a bob that she highlighted with random streaks of color. This month they were bright green. She blew a spiral lock out of her eyes and glanced at the group.

"What did I miss?" she asked.

"Andre was just telling us that the groom in the wedding he's going to used to torture him as a child," Nick said. "I think I may have to pay a surprise visit to the castle and bash him on the head with my umbrella."

"Why didn't you say anything before?" I asked. Andre shrugged. "And why, when you took their engagement photos, didn't you walk out or at least cancel the plan to have you be their wedding photographer?"

"Because Dooney—" Andre paused to collect himself. He stared at the door to the shop where Viv had just appeared.

"Dooney what?" Nick asked. "Don't keep us in suspense, love, we all want to know what happened."

Andre drew in a deep breath and exhaled it through his nose. "Dooney Portis didn't remember me."

We all blinked at him. Personally, I thought this was the best possible outcome and was a little bewildered by Andre's agitation.

"I'm failing to see the problem," Harry said. "I mean, isn't it good that he doesn't remember you?"

"You don't have to worry about him bullying you, yeah," Fee said.

Nick studied his partner closely. "Unless, you're struggling because his bullying was a significant chapter in your life but for him, as evidenced by him not remembering you, it was nothing."

"Exactly!" Andre cried. "How could he have been so cruel and then have just forgotten about me?"

"Because Dooney Portis is a horrible person," Viv said as she joined us. "That's who you're talking about, isn't it?"

"How did you guess?" Andre asked.

"I met him a few times when Piper started dating him," Viv said. "He was very handsy, and all I could think was how could Piper tie her life to a man who had such a ridiculous nickname and who felt free to grope anyone who came within reach. Gross."

"It is ridiculous and he is gross," Andre said. He looked as if the thought cheered him immensely.

"He's an absolute wastrel," Viv said. "I have no idea what she sees in him."

"His parents' social connections, no doubt," Harry said. He reached out and grabbed my hand, pulling me close. "I'm betting theirs is not a love match."

Then he kissed me. I felt my face go warm, knowing that my friends were likely grinning and rolling their eyes as one.

When he pulled back and my brain started to function again, I looked at Andre and said, "Don't you worry. I'll have your back all weekend. I won't let him anywhere near you on the off chance he remembers who you are."

Andre smiled. "Thanks, Scarlett."

"And if you need backup, you can call me and Harrison," Nick said. "We can be there in a little over an hour."

"Speaking of which, we'd better be off," Harry said. "I have to drop off the three of you and then get back here in time to walk Bella, or who knows what havoc she will wreak on our flat."

"You can always leave her with me," Fee said. "I'm staying in Scarlett's old room for the weekend so I'm here all day every day."

"I'll keep that in mind," Harrison said.

"Are you sure you don't mind tending the shop alone?" Viv asked. "Saturday's market can be a lot."

"Oh, I won't be alone," Fee said. She tossed her head flirtatiously. "I have a friend from millinery school helping me out."

"Wonderful," I said. "If she likes it, maybe we can consider hiring her. We need the help."

"*He* might be looking for more regular income," Fee said.

We all turned to stare at her in surprise.

"Fiona Felton, are you holding out on us?" Nick cried. "Do you have a beau?"

"Maybe." She giggled.

"I feel less and less bad about leaving you alone," Viv said.

"Same," I agreed. I gave Fee a quick hug and a wink. "Have fun."

With some mild cursing, Harry managed to fit my bags and Viv's and Andre's into the boot, using all of his body weight to shut it. Then he hustled us into the car. Because neither Viv nor I owned a car and Andre's was too small, Harry was driving us out to Sussex and then would pick us up the day after the wedding. Yes, the man had the title of best fiancé in the entire world locked down.

Viv fell asleep in the backseat while Andre stared out the window with his earbuds in as he listened to an audiobook. I was in the passenger seat beside Harry, and I decided to take the opportunity to discover my man's expectations for our wedding. We'd gotten engaged over a year ago, but because of the pandemic, we'd had to delay our plans, and now we were having a hard time committing to anything. We couldn't seem to move forward and had yet to pick a day or a venue or anything, really. I wondered if this was a bad sign, like maybe we didn't really want to get married.

"What's your feeling about a castle wedding?" I asked. Might as well jump in with both feet, I figured.

"Depends," he said. "Do I have to wear a kilt?"

"Do you want to wear a kilt?"

"I don't think I have the knees for it," he said.

"You have fine knees," I countered. "But aren't you supposed to be Scottish to wear a kilt?"

"I am Scottish as a matter of fact," he said.

I blinked. "How did I not know this before now?"

"You never asked."

I wondered what else I had neglected to ask him. Suddenly, I didn't think we knew each other as well as we should if we were going to get married.

His hand closed over mine on the console between us. His palm was warm, and he gently squeezed my fingers.

"Of course we do," he said.

"We do what?"

"Know each other well enough to get married," he said. "That's what you were thinking, weren't you?"

"How do you know what I was thinking?" I asked.

"Because I watched you for years just waiting for you to notice me," he said. "And not in a creepy way, but in a I-have-a-mad-crush-on-this-girl way, and I think I'm pretty good at guessing what you're thinking after all those years of observation."

"No doubt," I said. I stared at him in wonder. It hit me like that sometimes—that this man was going to be my husband. I had no idea how I'd gotten so lucky, but I definitely didn't want to jinx it.

Our relationship had originally gotten off to a rocky start. When we were kids, terrorizing Notting Hill with our shenanigans in a pack of unruly shopkeepers' children, I had noticed Harry and considered him a friend but was too busy having crushes on older boys to pay him much attention. After Mim passed away, I didn't come back to London for years. It was too hard to face the hat shop without her. When I did return at Viv's insistence, Harry was very suspicious about the sort of person I'd become. That whole viral party-crasher thing certainly didn't help my image.

It took me a while to thaw him out, but I'd always loved a good challenge, and much to my surprise and delight, we fell in love. So many good things had happened to me since I returned to England, I had to believe that this was where I was meant to be all along.

"Why are you looking at me like that?" he asked.

"Like what?"

"I'm not sure," he said. "I can't tell if you love me quite desperately or if you're afraid you're allergic to me."

"The first one," I said, knowing he was teasing me. "Definitely, the first one."

"I love that look," he said. His voice was full of tenderness. "At the risk of sounding proprietary, I like to think that look is just for me, that you'll never look at anyone else quite like that."

I wouldn't. I couldn't. I'd never loved anyone as much as I loved Harrison Wentworth. In fact, feelings of this magnitude made me think a castle wedding might be required. As if we needed a building that big just to hold all of my feelings for this man.

My heart was so full I thought it might burst. Instead of suffocating him with my affection, I rested my head on his shoulder. He immediately leaned his cheek against the top of my head.

"I don't care where we get married, Ginger, and if you decide that it's a castle you want," he said. "Then it's a castle you'll get."

Well, didn't that make my inner Disney princess swoon. A castle. I tried to picture it. It wasn't as hard as you might think. As we left the city behind and headed south toward Brighton and the English Channel, I closed my eyes and let my imagination run wild, trying to picture myself as a bride in a castle. In my mind, it was a beautiful spring day, the sun was warm, the breeze was cool, my dress was white, and I stood on the parapet, looking over the countryside. I half expected a robin to land on my outstretched hand and sing me a happy tune.

"Ginger, we're here." Harry's voice was a low growl in my ear.

I burrowed against him, not wanting to wake up just yet. What had begun as a daydream about our wedding had turned into a full-on nap. My eyes felt gritty and my mouth was dry. I wasn't positive but I thought there might be some dried-up drool in the corner of my lips. I glanced at Harry in alarm. He smiled.

"Still love you," he said.

I grinned. "I love you, too. How long was I out?"

"You clocked out at the halfway point and slept through until I parked the car. Look." He gestured out the window, and I turned and took in the sight of the massive medieval castle that loomed over the surrounding landscape like a sleeping giant.

"Whoa," Viv said from the backseat. "Now I know why Piper was fine with having us join her wedding weekend. This place is colossal. You could lose somebody in there if you weren't careful."

"There are one hundred and twenty rooms," Andre read from a glossy brochure that featured Waverly Castle on the front. "Five acres of gardens, stables and a manmade lake."

"I wonder if we could just move in," I said. "We could keep moving rooms, stay ahead of the cleaning staff, and they'd never even know we were there."

"In our youth, we absolutely would have tried that," Viv said. She patted Harry on the shoulder. "Can't you see the old gang pulling a stunt like that?"

"Sure, except that Dean would have ratted us out to the first adult he saw," he said.

"And Chester would have eaten all the food in the kitchen," I said. "He never met a sandwich he didn't feel the need to consume."

Viv and Harry laughed, while Andre nodded. He'd heard us discuss our childhood friends before.

"Despite my dislike of the wilderness," Andre said, "the castle and surrounding countryside will make for some incredible photos."

He climbed out of the car and we all followed. Harry had parked in the circular drive at the entrance to the massive stone edifice. There were several other cars parked nearby but I paid them no mind as I took in the building before us. Coming from the United States, I was left slack-jawed and wide-eyed because castles were just not the norm there, and I tried to process that people had actually lived and worked and birthed in this place that had been built over one thousand years ago. Mind blown.

There are said to be over four thousand castles in England, and while I could think of several impressive residences in the United States, there wasn't a smattering of castles across the countryside and definitely nothing as old as this. There just wasn't.

I wondered again if I could handle getting married in a castle. Now that I was here, staring up at the intimidating structure, it seemed like a no. A White Castle burger joint sure, but this, no, this was too much.

"Viv, darling," a voice called from the front doors of the castle.

Piper May stood there in another haute couture outfit, this one a pair of multicolored striped capri pants with a bright blue bolero-style jacket over a white silk blouse. She was wearing sandals and hurried down the steps toward us. And by "us," I mean Viv, because Piper did not seem to care that the rest of us were here.

"Viv, your timing is amazing," Piper cried. The two women air hugged and kissed. I glanced at Harrison to see what he made of that. He frowned, looking confused. He wasn't alone there. What was the point of hugging someone if you didn't actually hug them? There wasn't one.

"The girls were just saying we should have a hen because it's two days before the wedding and when I told them that you were coming, they went mad. Everyone wants you to join in."

Viv shrugged out of her pale pink cashmere cardigan,

letting it slide down her arms. She draped it over her forearm with the grace of a runway model. Then she lowered her sunglasses and studied Piper over the top of her shades.

"I don't *hen*," she said.

With that, she walked around Piper, leaving her bags to the valet who had come rushing outside.

"What does that mean?" Piper turned and asked the rest of us. "She doesn't hen. Everyone hens. The hen party is the pinnacle of female bonding before a girl gets married."

"You know Viv," I said. "She doesn't do things 'just because.'"

"Well, that's completely unacceptable," Piper said. "Do you have any idea what a coup it is for me to have the reclusive Vivian Tremont here for the entire wedding weekend? Come along, Andre, help me change her mind."

Andre looked like he'd protest, but Piper was stronger than she appeared. She put her arm through his and dragged him after Viv. Halfway up the wide staircase, she swung around and cried, "Good to see you, Harrison. You're as delicious as ever." Then she gave him a very significant look that I found I did not like at all. Was there some history there that I didn't know about? I turned slowly to face my fiancé.

"So, you didn't mention that you know Piper May," I said. I was fishing, absolutely. How the man didn't hear the line spool out from the reel, I have no idea.

"I assumed you knew," he said.

"How would I know that?"

"I thought Viv would have mentioned it," he said. "We

all ran around in the same post-university set in London. It's not as big a city as you'd think for twentysomethings."

"Twentysomethings on the prowl," I said.

Harry threw back his head and laughed. "Is that why your nose is in a crinkle? You think I had a thing with Piper."

"No, I don't. Did you?" I asked. "Because when I met her for the first time, she was very interested in knowing how I bagged you."

"Bagged?" he asked. "Like I'm a head of cauliflower at the market?"

I shrugged.

"It's more like I bagged you," he said.

"So, I'm the cauliflower?" I asked. Of course, I was secretly pleased that he saw it the same way I did.

"Excuse me, miss." A valet paused beside us. "Ms. May told me to inform you that you'll be sharing the blue suite with Ms. Tremont."

"Oh, thank you," I said. The poor man was dressed in a forest green uniform and reminded me of a bellhop as he gathered my bags. I felt as if I ought to help him, but before I could, Harry slipped him a folded pound note of a large denomination as a tip, and the man bobbed his head and shot off with the bags, tottering a bit as he went.

"Do you know the history of Waverly Castle?" Harry asked.

"Are you trying to change the subject?" I asked.

"That depends. Is it working?" He took my hand in his and walked me not to the main entrance but through a stone arc that led into a garden overflowing with blooms of every color.

"Wow." I breathed in the heady floral perfume, feeling as if I'd walked through a doorway to an enchanted land. I could see why Piper wanted to have her ceremony here. The princess vibe was strong.

"Breathtaking," Harry said. I turned and he was staring at me. Charmer. It still wasn't going to let him off the hook.

"So, about you and Piper," I said. I strolled down a gravel path, leaving him to follow.

He let out a heavy sigh and said, "You're a bird dog, Ginger."

I stopped abruptly and faced the castle as I assumed a pointer position with one hand jutting toward the building as I stared at its thick stone walls.

"All right, I surrender," he said, "The truth is, yes, Piper and I dated."

Chapter 3

"You actually dated her?" I asked. I was incredulous. I couldn't imagine a woman less suited to Harry, but I think what had me perplexed was more the idea that my Harry had willingly spent time with someone as superficial as Piper. I resumed walking, turning left onto a narrow path. Harry joined me and we found ourselves in a secluded alcove with a bench and a shallow lily pond.

"We only went out once," he explained. "No, that's inaccurate. It was twice. Those were two of the longest dates of my life."

As if exhausted by the mere memory, he slumped down on the stone bench, pulling me with him.

"Poor Harry," I said. I rested my head on his shoulder and he wrapped his arm around me, tucking me up against him. "I won't badger you anymore. I am selfishly relieved that you did not find your match in that woman."

"No, but I feel compelled to clarify that she dumped me before I had the chance to end things between us."

"She dumped *you*?" I was outraged.

A startled magpie protested my outburst and erupted out of a nearby bush, flapping up into the sky with a flash of its black-and-white feathers.

"Yes," he said. "She said something about her return on investment not being sustainable with me."

"Meaning you were too poor for her," I said. I felt bluntness was required.

"More accurately, yes," he said.

"Well, I'm betting she regrets that now," I said. "Now she's marrying Dooney, whom I despise on principle. Anyone who could bully Andre has to be a horrible person."

"Obviously," he said. "Although this marriage could be a real love match between two shallow, self-interested, vapid people, and if you think about it, they're saving some innocent souls by marrying each other."

"That does put a positive spin on it," I said. We admired the afternoon sunlight on the side of the castle. The breeze that swept through the gardens lifted strands of my hair, teasing the ends. It was a glorious day and, according to the weather forecast, it was going to be a perfect weekend.

"I wish you could stay for the wedding," I said. "I'm going to miss you."

"I'll miss you, too." He paused and then added, "Try not to get into trouble while you're here."

"You say that as if I actively look for less-than-desirable situations," I protested.

"You do have a knack," he said.

I knew there was no arguing the point. Weirdly, over the past few years, I'd had the misfortune to stumble across a number of dead bodies. I think it was because being an American, I was an outsider and I noticed things that others missed. That's what I told myself at any rate.

"It's a wedding. I'll be fine." He looked dubious, so I raised my right hand and said, "I promise I won't get into any untoward predicaments. At least, I'll try not to."

"That's not as reassuring as you might think," he said.

A frown appeared between his eyebrows and I reached up and massaged it away with my thumb. I leaned in close and kissed him quick.

"Don't worry. I'll be too busy checking out the castle from top to bottom as a possible venue for our wedding to think of anything else," I said. My gaze moved back to the castle walls that seemed to loom over us. "Now go ahead and tell me about its history."

Harrison's lips curved up. "Now you're trying to distract me."

"Not entirely," I said. "I really want to know. If we decide to get married here, I don't want to find out that it's the scene of a massacre or some other horror. That would be a terrible way to start a marriage, making our vows on top of the graves of the slain."

"Well, it's over a thousand years old, so there's likely some history here that isn't pretty," he said.

JENN McKINLAY

"Why do you suppose Waverly Castle has survived when so many other castles have fallen to ruin?" I asked.

"Because the family who owns it, the Mulvaneys, opened it decades ago for tours and events like Piper's wedding," he said. "Can you even imagine trying to staff a place this large if you were the nobleman who owned it? It would hemorrhage money."

"Having tourists and events to keep it operating in the black is smart," I said. "I wonder what the original residents would make of that?"

"I think the original residents would be shocked by how magnificent it is. It certainly didn't start out that way. At the time it was built, it was to compete with Arundel Castle in West Sussex. Both were established during the reign of Edward the Confessor," he said.

"Okay, see, we don't have names like that for old dead guys in America," I said.

"Old dead guys?" Harry repeated, sounding like he was choking back a laugh. "He was our king."

I shrugged and said, "Still old and dead. Tell me more."

"About Edward or the castle?" He stood up and pulled me to my feet. Taking my hand in his, we continued our walk through the garden.

"Edward, of course," I said. "I mean, while the castle is lovely, I really need to know why he was called 'the Confessor.'"

"Understandable," Harry said. "Besides, there's likely a tour of the castle that could tell you more than I ever could, but Edward the Confessor, that I can cover. Edward was born in 1003 and was one of the last Anglo-Saxon kings of England."

"Yes, yes, whatever." I rolled my hand in a *get on with it* gesture. "But what did he confess? What did he get up to as king?"

"You're going to be disappointed," he said. "Edward didn't confess anything, not really. He was canonized by Pope Alexander III but because he wasn't martyred like his uncle, Edward the Martyr, he was dubbed Edward the Confessor."

"Hmm. Not nearly as salacious as I'd hoped," I said.

"He was known for his piety, so salaciousness was unlikely."

"Didn't William the Conqueror take over the throne after him?" I asked.

Harry looked impressed. "You've been reading up."

"Some kings you remember more than others. Conqueror sticks in the brain more than Confessor." I glanced at the castle. "No offense to Edward."

Harry laughed. "The passing of Edward is one of those historical crossroads where everything changed, developing both feudalism and manorialism, the intertwining of the French and English cultures, and the commissioning of the Domesday Book."

"Oh, I've heard about that," I said. "That's the book William the Conqueror commissioned so that he could raise taxes for his army by determining how wealthy his subjects were right down to the eggs in the henhouse."

"I've read bits of it, and it's actually fascinating to see

how people worked and survived at the time," Harry said. He gestured to the castle. "Just think, you're going to be sleeping in the same castle where generations of nobility and their servants have lived and died."

I stopped walking and stared up at the thick stone walls. They glowed softly in the golden afternoon light. People had died in there. I wasn't sure why this hadn't occurred to me before, but it hadn't.

"This place is definitely haunted," I said. I don't know what it said about my character that this actually thrilled me, but I was ridiculously excited to get inside and poke around.

"I've only heard stories of one ghost," Harry said. "A woman, if I remember right. I can't remember how she died but she's said to haunt the castle to this day."

"I wonder if I'll see her," I said. The thought gave me a delicious shiver.

"Oh, no," Harry said. He shook his head and pulled me close. "You just promised not to get into trouble."

"Well, I can't help it if the place is haunted," I said. I looped my arms around his neck. "I mean, ghosts are gonna ghost, you know?"

"Now you're going to have to ring me a couple of times a day," he said. "Just so I know you're all right."

"Of course," I agreed. "After all, I'll need updates on Bella. I know she's a daddy's girl but I would like to think she'll miss me at least a little."

"She will," he said. "And I will, too."

Harry planted a lingering kiss on my mouth. It was just

tipping into inappropriate in public when an angry voice broke through the passionate haze.

"How dare you?" a woman's voice cried.

I froze with my mouth against Harry's. At first, I thought it was Piper chewing me out for kissing Harry, her former whatever, never mind that I was now engaged to the man. But the voice wasn't right. It was shrill and defensive and scared.

"You can't do this to me! It will ruin everything, everything. Is that what you want? To expose me?"

Harry, who had also gone still, broke the kiss and peered down at me in alarm. He jerked his head in the opposite direction of where the yelling was taking place, which was the other side of the thick rose arbor.

A man's voice, indiscernible apart from its masculine tone, responded to the woman, sounding curt. Whatever he'd said, the woman was not having it.

"I will see you in hell first," she snapped.

I would have lingered to hear more but Harry grabbed my hand and led me away in the opposite direction, out of the gardens and through a copse of trees as if we were fleeing a crime scene. To be fair, for my understated Englishman, I'm sure overhearing the argument was akin to witnessing a murder.

"Well, someone's weekend is off to a rocky start," he said as we strode along a well-worn path that led over a wooden bridge that arced over a narrow brook.

"Do you suppose there are other events happening here this weekend?" I asked. "I mean, I know Piper rented out

47

the entire castle, but the grounds are big enough for a circus to come through and not be noticed."

Harry hesitated and then said, "I don't think Piper is the type to share—even things she's not using."

"Got it," I said. That meant that whoever the woman was, she had to be involved in Piper's wedding somehow. Interesting.

We continued to hurry through the woods until I was positive we were going to get lost and they'd have to send out a search party for us.

"Harry, slow down," I said. "It's not like anyone is chasing us."

"But there was drama," he said. He made it sound as if it were something that was contagious like the flu and we had to outrun it.

"Yes, and instead of bolting, we could have lingered and heard more," I said. "Now I'm going to spend all weekend wondering who was bickering and why."

"But that would have been rude," he said.

I stared at him. Truly, I was boggled by his definition of bad manners sometimes. We broke through the trees and found ourselves on the far side of the castle.

"How do we get back to the entrance of the castle from here?" I asked. "Because it feels like we are miles from where we need to be."

The trees had opened up to a steep hill on top of which sat a circular tower, which formed one end of the castle. Man, this place was huge.

There were flower beds planted all along the base of the hill and several trellises with vines twining around them. Their leaves had started to unfurl and their fat buds were plump and nearly ready to open. Behind one trellis I saw what appeared to be a wooden door.

"Where do you suppose that goes?" I asked.

Harry stepped forward and stared at the door. He shrugged. "Back to the castle."

"Let's go in," I said.

"What? No, we have no idea what's in there," he protested.

"Aw, come on, Harry, live a little," I said. "It's an adventure."

I didn't wait for his answer but stepped behind the trellis and reached for the doorknob.

"Scarlett, wait," he said. "What if that's where they keep their pet tiger or lion?"

I stared at him. "I'm sure they do not have any big cats on the premises."

"Alligator?"

"Do you even have those in England?"

"Well, no, but . . . here, at least let me go first so if there is something, I can die like a good fiancé, trying to save you," he said.

Oh, I did love this man. I stepped aside. He took out his phone and put the light on. It felt very Nancy Drew to find a secret passageway into the castle. Then again, it might not be a *secret* passageway, but I didn't want to quibble with my imagination.

"Stay close," he said.

I pressed up against his back as he pulled the door open. It didn't creak but opened smoothly as if it was frequently used. Huh. He shone the light inside, and we discovered a clean tunnel with a light switch set into the wall beside the door. I flicked it on and wall sconces flickered to life, lighting the entire length of the passageway.

"Is it wrong that this disappoints?" I asked.

"No," he said. "I was hoping for something dark and dank myself. This seems like a well-used shortcut for the staff."

"I'm sure no one will mind if we use it now," I said. Harry put his phone away and took my hand. The tunnel was just wide enough for us to walk side by side.

"Do you suppose this was an old smuggler's tunnel?" I asked. "Someone importing brandy into the castle? Or maybe an escape route for a man of the cloth fleeing religious persecution?"

"Could be any of those things," he said. "I'm sure someone at the castle can tell us."

The passageway ended at a flight of stairs. We exchanged a look. Should we? Shouldn't we? I shrugged. We'd come this far.

I began the trek up the steep stone steps. There was no handrail, so I stayed close to the wall. I could feel Harry behind me. It didn't occur to me until we reached the landing that we had no idea where the door opened up to, if the door opened at all. It could be locked. My hands started to sweat.

I reached for the door handle and it turned. Phew! I didn't want to walk all the way back and around the exterior of the castle. The door opened into a room, and I poked my head around it to see where we'd landed.

A severe-looking man was standing in front of the door with his arms folded over his chest and a frown marring his face. At least, I assumed he was frowning. It was hard to tell behind the bushy red beard.

"Oh, hello," I said. I stepped into the room, making room for Harry to follow. At a glance, I realized we were in a library. The walls were covered in floor-to-ceiling shelves of books. The large space was filled with rows of shorter shelves, packed with more volumes. The tops of the waist-high bookcases had thick-spined books on display in wooden holders and busts of what I assumed were famous authors. I desperately wanted to examine the books and the busts, but the man in front of me stopped me in my tracks.

"Cheers," Harry greeted the man. The bearded man's frown deepened.

"What were you doing in there?" the man demanded. He was dressed in wellies, cargo pants and a well-worn flannel shirt. He spoke in such a thick brogue that it took me a minute to decipher his Scots. He was tall and broad and looked like he'd have no trouble tossing us like a caber. Judging by the look on his face, he was giving it a fair amount of consideration.

Uh-oh.

Chapter 4

"You're not another bloody ghost hunter, are you?" the man asked.

Harry and I exchanged a look. *Ghost hunter?*

I gave the stranger my best people-pleasing smile. He remained unmoved. I tried a hair toss to see if that could distract him. Nope.

"I'm sorry, we're here for the May-Portis wedding and while we were touring the grounds, we got turned around," I said. "We found the door on the other end of the castle and thought it might be a shortcut, and it was."

"It is for the staff of castle Waverly only," the man snapped. He gestured to the door we'd just come through, and I turned to see a *Staff Only* sign on the front of it.

"Apologies," Harry said. "There wasn't a sign on the door at the other end."

The man pursed his lips and paused to consider that. "Fair enough. I'm Archie Carlton, castle caretaker, and I'd appreciate it if you'd stay out of the staff areas from now on."

By "appreciate" I figured he meant that he'd be even scarier should we have to have this conversation again. Duly noted.

"Why did you think we were ghost hunters?" I asked. I felt Harry's gaze on my face, and I was certain he would have preferred that I just let it go. Yeah, not gonna happen.

"Because there's always someone poking around looking for the McKenna bride where they're not supposed to," he said.

"The McKenna bride, is that what the ghost is called?" Harry asked. I glanced at him in surprise. That was going to be my next question, but he scooped me, and here I thought he wasn't interested.

"Aye, she was the daughter of Laird McKenna," Archie said. His brogue seemed to get thicker with the telling. "She was supposed to marry Baron Mulvaney, who resided in the castle at the time, but she died tragically before the wedding. It's said she haunts the castle in her bridal garb to this day."

A shiver rippled up my spine with icy fingers. We were in a haunted castle. I could not wait to tell Viv.

Mr. Carlton's face grew cautious and he said, "The Waverly Castle Society doesn't like the staff to talk about the ghost. They feel it misrepresents the history of the place. I'd appreciate it if you didn't mention this conversation to anyone."

I nodded and said, "Of course, we understand completely. Nice to meet you, Mr. Carlton."

A low grumble in his throat was his only response. Harry and I hurried out of the library without a chance to look around. Darn it.

We were in the bowels of the castle, but Harry must have had some swank ancestors in his family history because he navigated the long corridors, full of antiques and art, as if he were born to it, and we soon found ourselves at the front of the castle. We slipped through the great room, which I barely glanced at, and out the front door.

I was trying to appear casual, but my posture was definitely similar to that of an escaping convict. Harry was much cooler than me. He strode down the steps as if he belonged there. How did he do that? Being an American had my impostor syndrome raging.

Harry took me in his arms for an emphatic kiss and a comforting hug. I could have stayed like that all night. When he released me, he held me by the upper arms, stared into my eyes and said, "I would never tell you what to do, but it occurs to me that you might consider avoiding Archie Carlton and the 'staff only' tunnel. And I definitely think you want to avoid doing any ghost hunting."

"Don't you worry," I said. I smoothed his shirt over his shoulders. "I am sufficiently freaked out by the forbidding Scotsman to not venture where I don't belong."

The corner of Harry's lips ticked up. "So, if I speak in a brogue, you might listen to my warnings more?"

I laughed. "I'm more likely to ask you to put on a kilt and let me take advantage of you."

Harry blew out a breath and his face turned a delightful shade of pink. "You're something, Scarlett Parker, you know that?"

"So, I've been told," I said. I kissed him quick and released him.

"Be good," he said.

"Always."

Harry strolled to his parked car, and I waved to him from the bottom of the steps, feeling a bit forlorn as I watched him disappear down the tree-lined drive. It was getting close to teatime and the afternoon was turning cool. I pulled my sweater sleeves down over my hands and crossed my arms over my chest.

I knew I had better get inside and check on Viv and Andre. Piper had seemed determined to have Viv join her hen, but Viv was not one to do something she didn't want to do—vast understatement there—and things could get tense if Piper got pushy.

There was a butler waiting at the large main door who hadn't been there a moment ago. I was relieved to see him, because I knew he could tell me where to find the suite that Viv and I were sharing. He was tall and thin, with neatly trimmed sideburns and a mustache that perched just above his upper lip. He wore a black suit with a white dress shirt and a narrow black tie. His shoes were shined to such mirrored perfection that I was certain I could check my lipstick in them if need be.

"Ms. Parker, good afternoon," he said. His voice was

low and distinct and very proper. "I'm Mr. Jenkins, the castle's head of staff, at your service."

My mouth popped open. How did he know my name?

"Your cousin, Ms. Tremont, mentioned that you would be arriving at any moment, and asked me to direct you to the blue suite," he said.

"She described my hair, didn't she?" I asked.

A small smile tipped the right corner of his lips. "She did give a very apt description of you."

Ah, the British gift of tact. It really was their superpower.

"Very thoughtful of her." I wondered what else she'd said, but I didn't think he'd tell me if I asked. His impeccable manners wouldn't allow it.

"If you'll follow me," he said. "Your bags have already been brought up to your room."

He gestured for me to step inside with a sweep of his arm and I did so, gaining my second glimpse of the enormous great hall and the interior of Waverly Castle. Wowza! How had I missed it the first time? Oh, yeah, I'd had my gaze fastened on the floor as Harry and I scuttled out like criminals.

Even in my wildest imaginings, I could not have conjured up this space. There were tapestries, incredibly detailed and massive, hanging on the walls. The fireplace was so big and broad, I could have walked right into it and stood at my full height. Me! And I'm not short.

The floors were polished stone with enormous carpets strewn about, and then there were the paintings. Generations of residents of Waverly Castle stared down at us

57

from their gilded frames, their lips set in tight brittle lines, their tiny noses turned up ever so slightly, their eyes cold and hard. Maybe I was imagining it but it felt as if they did not approve of the modern use of their home.

Mr. Jenkins closed the door and neatly stepped around me. A staircase, also made of stone, swept up one side of the great room and he started up, leaving me to follow. Along the wall were more portraits of disapproving expressions. I kept my eyes averted, not wanting to see any of these faces in my dreams tonight.

"Tea will be delivered to your suite at four o'clock and dinner will be served in the dining room at eight," he said. "Ms. Tremont mentioned that you and Mr. Eisel would be joining her for tea?"

He posed the statement as a question, obviously looking for confirmation.

"Yes, absolutely," I said. I marveled a bit that Viv had acclimated to castle life so quickly that she had already issued orders to the butler. I was positive I wouldn't ask the man for so much as an umbrella during a rainstorm for the duration of our stay. Intimidated? Me? Yup.

At the top of the staircase was a long passageway that overlooked the great room below. Three corridors branched off it, and Mr. Jenkins turned at the last one, following it all the way to the end. He paused in front of a closed door and knocked three times.

"Come in," a voice I recognized as Viv's called out.

Mr. Jenkins opened the door for me and stepped back to allow me to enter.

"If you need anything, Ms. Parker, do not hesitate to ask," he said.

"I won't," I lied.

His lips twitched again in the corners as if he knew I was fibbing. For a second, I wondered what it would be like to grow up in a house like this. Was this what childhood had been like for Prince William and Prince Harry? Were there just people around all the time, making certain their every want and need was attended? How extraordinary.

I stepped into our suite and then halted. I was standing in a large sitting room that boasted a thick blue carpet and cream-colored furniture. Viv was reclined on a divan, looking like the fair maiden waiting to be rescued from the tower by a knight.

She was reading a book and didn't look up from the page when she spoke. "Your room is over there." She waved a hand in the direction of a doorway on the far side of the sitting room.

I crossed the room, curiosity quickening my pace. I pushed open the door and found a bedroom done in matching blue with a wardrobe, vanity and bed all made of heavy dark wood. Very castle-worthy. And the bed? It had curtains. Thick curtains that I could pull around the mattress like a big cocoon. I couldn't wait to go to sleep tonight.

There were two windows and I glanced outside to see the view. It was of the gardens. In fact, when I looked down, I could see the small lily pond where Harry and I had just been. It made me miss him all the more.

"Did you know that this castle was built at the time of Edward the Confessor?" I asked Viv as I reentered the sitting room.

"It was established then," Viv said. "But it was nothing like the building we're in now. It was a motte and bailey castle to start with."

I thought about pretending to know what she was talking about and just looking it up later, but I knew Viv wouldn't judge me for not knowing the intricacies of castles. As I had mentioned to Harry, castles were not something we had in America. McMansions, sure, but castles, not so much.

"Explain," I said.

"A motte is a raised piece of earth atop of which a wooden keep is built," Andre said as he entered the room. He had his camera in his hand and was fussing with a lens. "And a bailey is an enclosed courtyard that sits at the base of the motte, also constructed out of wood."

"Not exactly a fortress then," I said. I thought about the hill where Harry and I had found the door, and realized it must have been the original motte. I wondered if the secret tunnel was original, too.

"No, thus, making for a lot of raiding and pillaging," Viv said. "Small wonder our ancestors were always at war. It can't have been that hard to knock over a wooden fence."

Andre glanced up and raised his camera to his eye. He snapped a series of pictures of Viv. I knew they would be spectacular because Andre was amazing, but also because Viv had that elusive quality of being otherly, as if she wasn't really a part of this world. She was the only person I'd ever known, aside from Mim, who captivated both men and women equally.

Women wanted to be her and men wanted to date her. And Viv was completely oblivious to it all. She was so very much like Mim in that way. Both of them were artists through and through.

"Where is your room, Andre?" I asked. "Nearby?"

"Right next door," he said. "My room looks out over the garden like yours."

"Really?" I asked. "Did you happen to be looking out the window about twenty minutes ago? Because Harry and I were taking a stroll and we heard, well, not to gossip, but we heard a couple having an argument and I wonder if it was someone you'd recognized."

"Really?" He looked intrigued. "Sadly, I wasn't looking out the window then," he said. "I was doing wardrobe management."

I frowned in confusion.

"Hanging up my clothes so that they won't get wrinkled," he explained.

"Oh." I bit my lip. I knew I should probably do the same but I was curious about the couple Harry and I had heard arguing. I knew it hadn't been Piper, as I was certain I would have recognized her voice, and if I hadn't, Harry would have, given that he had dated her and all. Yes, I was still processing, which reminded me.

"Viv, why didn't you tell me that Harry had dated Piper?" I asked.

"What?" Andre's eyes went wide.

"I know, right?" I asked him.

Viv glanced up from her novel. She frowned at me. "I'm sure that can't be right."

"Oh, it's right," I said. "Harry told me so himself."

"Just now?" Viv asked.

"In the garden."

"What made him do that?" she asked. She lowered the book into her lap. "I mean, he's known about the wedding and that we were coming here for weeks. Why mention it now when it was really nothing?"

"It was the way Piper looked at him when she said hello to him," I said. "My ex-girlfriend radar went off and I asked him if there had been something between them. He said they went on two dates."

"Oh, pish tosh," Andre cried. "Two dates is nothing. It's that no-man's-land between acquaintance and friend. Clearly, she didn't even make the friend cut."

"No, she didn't," I agreed.

"What did Harrison say about it?" Viv asked.

"That they were the two most boring dates of his life," I said.

Viv laughed. "He got that right. Poor Piper is the most boring person I've ever known. That's why I'm refusing to do the hen party. I already know it will be deadly dull."

"Harsh," I said.

"Truth," she countered.

"So, tell us what you heard," Andre said. "We can study the other couples and place bets on who we think it is."

"And this wedding just got so much more interesting," Viv said. She beamed at us and I laughed.

"You two are terrible, but all right," I said. I recounted the argument for them.

"Not much to go on," Andre said. "It could have been staff having a disagreement."

"I suppose," I agreed. I wasn't convinced, however, and I was about to argue my case when a knock on the door interrupted me.

We all glanced at one another. Viv frowned. "I hope that's not Piper, coming round again."

I shrugged and crossed the room to open the door. I could run interference. I was good at that.

The handsome man standing in the hallway was unexpected. His dark hair fell over his forehead in thick waves. He was tall and trim, wearing designer clothes that fit his frame so perfectly I was certain they were bespoke. Normally, when I encountered a good-looking man, my default setting was to flirt. Not this time. There was a coldness in his brown eyes that made me back up a half step.

"May I help you?" I asked.

"Maybe," he said. He grinned. It was a slash of white that didn't reach his eyes. "I'm looking for Vivian."

"And you are?" I asked. I had a feeling I knew, but I wanted it confirmed.

"I'm the man of the hour, of course, Dooney Portis," he said.

Chapter 5

I don't usually take an *immediate* dislike to a person. In fact, I generally like everyone, even the grumpies, but there was something about this guy that set all my internal alarm bells to clanging. Maybe it was because I knew about his history with Andre or perhaps it was the side part in his hair or the overpowering scent of his Oud de Carthage cologne. Whatever it was, I didn't like him.

He took a step forward as if assured of his welcome, so I did what anyone would do in such a situation. I shut the door in his face.

"Just a minute," I yelled through the door. I whirled around and saw Viv staring at me with round eyes and Andre silently laughing.

"Did you just slam the door on him?" he asked, wheezing a bit.

"Yup." I looked at Viv. "Do you want to see him?"

She closed her book and set it aside. She studied her manicure. "I suppose I have to, given he's the groom and all." She turned to Andre and added, "But you don't. Feel free to leave through my bedroom if you want."

"Oh, I want," he said. He turned and walked to her bedroom, then paused in the doorway. "Unless you two need me?"

"Nah." I waved a dismissive hand at him. "We've got this."

He glanced between us and then nodded. "I'm right next door, bellow and I'll come running."

"Why does Piper's fiancé want to talk to you?" I asked Viv.

She shrugged. "I'm sure I have no idea and I won't know until you let him in."

I turned back to the door. I opened it, half hoping he'd gotten the hint and skulked away. No such luck. He was leaning against the doorframe as if he'd known it was only a matter of time before I invited him in. Annoying.

"Sorry, I had to make sure everyone was decent. Viv's in here." I stepped back, opening the door wide.

Dooney sauntered into the room and I turned to follow him, leaving the door open. I don't know why, maybe it was being in a castle, but it felt very wrong to be entertaining a strange gentleman in our suite. Then again, it could be the bad vibe I was getting off him.

"Hello, Vivian," he said. He crossed the room to where

she sat. I noticed Viv didn't get up to greet him. There was no smile on her face or friendly, exuberant hug—just her cool, assessing stare.

"Dooney." She propped her chin in her hand, looking bored. "How are you?"

"Never better," he said. "I'm finally living my best life. At long last, I'm going to have more money than I know what to do with."

"Good for you," Viv said. There was a tiny edge of disdain to her voice but he didn't appear to hear it.

"I was surprised you agreed to design the hats for Piper's bridesmaids," he said. "Generous of you, given the circumstances."

"Circumstances?" Viv repeated. Her eyebrows lowered in an expression of confusion.

"Why, yes," he said. He gestured between them. "I know you had a terrible time getting over me."

Viv's mouth dropped open. She blinked twice. "Getting over you?"

"Oh, come on, Viv," he cajoled. "Everyone knows you fancied me back in the day."

"Fancied you?" She kept repeating him as if she couldn't believe the ridiculous things he was saying. Her expression was one of amazement. If Dooney had declared himself king of England, Viv couldn't have looked more stunned.

"Yes, of course," he said. "That's why you always got that look on your face whenever I was around."

"This look?" Viv asked. Then she made an expression that if you knew her, you would know was one of utmost

JENN McKINLAY

contempt. Her nostrils flared, her eyes narrowed, and her lip curled just the tiniest bit. It wasn't a full sneer, but the intent was there.

"Yes, exactly." Dooney clapped his hands. "I noticed that you only ever looked at *me* that way. Quite endearing, really."

"There's only one part of that sentence that you got right," Viv said. "That's your look all right, but it doesn't mean I fancy you. Rather it indicates—"

"She admires your aesthetic," I said.

They both turned to look at me with identical expressions of incredulity.

"His aesthetic?" Viv asked. Her nose crinkle deepened.

"What does that even mean?" Dooney asked.

"Your sense of style," I said. Viv rolled her eyes. I took Dooney's preening expression as confirmation that I'd played the right card.

"Is that so, Viv?" he asked.

I stared at her from behind him, making my eyes huge and imploring. I didn't want her to offend him and get us kicked out of the castle before I had a proper chance to poke around. She gave me an annoyed look.

"You certainly have a distinctive style," Viv said.

"That fascinates you," he purred.

I checked my gag reflex. Poor Viv. What had I done? I tried to think of a way to get rid of him.

"Well, so long as you're not here because you're pining for me, there won't be any problems with the wedding," he said.

"Pining?" she repeated. I think it was sheer force of

68

will that kept her from rolling her eyes. "What sort of problems did you imagine would happen?"

"Oh, nothing really," he said. He shrugged. "Piper has been concerned that you might design hideous hats for the bridesmaids, you know, out of bitterness that I'm marrying her and not you."

"Did Piper say that?" I asked quickly, before Viv could voice her opinion, which likely would have rendered him bloody. Also, I thought he was lying. It seemed unlikely that Piper would say such a thing given how desperate she was to have Viv design the hats to begin with.

Dooney swung around and looked me over from head to foot, pausing on my red hair—yes, the bias against gingers is real. "She mentioned you, too. The 'party crasher' she called you."

I didn't so much as blink. Instead, I gave him a small smile and said, "Nicknames. What can you do, *Dooney*?"

His eyes narrowed as if he was trying to decide if I was mocking him or not. I was. Thankfully, there was a knock on the door and Viv called, "Come in."

Two castle staff, in black-and-white uniforms, wheeled a tray into the room.

"Tea's here!" Viv cried. She glanced at Dooney. "We'd ask you to stay but I'm sure Piper will be looking for you. Ta-ta!"

Dooney looked confused. I doubted he got rushed out of places very often. I moved to hold the door open for him while our tea was set up on a small table by the window.

"Nice to meet you," I said. "See you at dinner tonight."

"Sure, I guess," he said. He looked grumpy, as if he hadn't gotten what he wanted out of this encounter, and sulked his way out of the room. I shut the door behind him and turned to Viv and asked, "What was that all about?"

She jerked her head in the direction of our tea servers and said, "I have no idea."

In other words, she wasn't going to say anything in front of the hired help. Smart woman. We waited quietly until the two women finished their task.

"Just leave your things outside the door when you're done, miss, and we'll collect them," the taller one said.

"Thank you very much," Viv said.

"Yes, thank you," I echoed. I opened the door to allow them to leave and shut and locked it behind them.

Viv was on her phone. "I'm texting Andre to let him know the tea is here."

"No need," he said. Andre returned through the door to Viv's room. "I almost left but then I didn't feel right leaving you at the mercy of Dooney. Just in case he was his usual obnoxious self, which he was, I wanted to be on hand, so I waited in your room. Nice view you've got there."

"You're a good friend, Andre," I said. "Dooney is awful and I'd think that even if I didn't know about your time with him at school."

"Not only is he awful, he's clearly delusional," Viv said. She rose from the divan and crossed the room to the small table by the window. She sat down and lifted the lid on the teapot to see that the tea had steeped sufficiently, and then poured three cups. Andre and I joined her at the table, and I immediately investigated the three-tiered tray of food the kitchen staff had prepared for tea.

There were the scones on the bottom, tiny finger sandwiches in the middle and petit fours on the top. My sweet tooth wanted to start at the top but a scone with raspberry jam and clotted cream wasn't a hardship, so I started there.

Using tongs, I selected my scone and passed the utensil to Andre. The scones were warm. I forgot all about Dooney and settled in with my light meal and marveled that I was enjoying high tea in a castle just like the heroine of every historical romance I had ever read. In short, I was having a moment.

"Are you all right, Scarlett?" Viv asked.

"Just soaking it all in," I said. I opened my eyes and took a bracing sip of tea.

"It is very posh, isn't it," Andre agreed.

"What do you suppose dinner will be like?" I asked.

"From what Piper said, there will be about fifty guests in total, formal attire required, and it's to be served in one of the dining rooms," Viv said.

"*One* of the dining rooms," I repeated. I nibbled my scone and pondered castle life. "How many dining rooms do you suppose there are?"

"More than anyone needs," Andre said. "While I appreciate the historic significance of the castle, I can't wrap my mind around the arrogance of building such a massive thing."

"But back in the day, it wasn't arrogance," Viv said. "It was survival."

I glanced between them. As an American, I had no dog in this fight and no opinion on castles other than—wow.

"How do you figure that?" Andre asked.

"The noblemen of the time had to provide employment for entire towns, in addition to lodgings for their own personal armies to ward off enemies. It wasn't like you could just apply online for jobs."

"Fair point," Andre said. "I'll admit that I'm looking at it through a modern lens but it's all just a bit much."

"Oh, definitely," Viv agreed. "No one needs this sort of wealth these days. It's obscene, which is precisely why it appeals to Piper."

"Status symbol?" I asked.

"Which is exactly why she's marrying Dooney," Viv said. "His family is as old as, well, Waverly Castle."

"Really?" I asked. "That's hard to believe. I mean I'd expect him to be more . . ."

"Learned, interesting, philanthropic?" Andre asked.

"Yes," I said. "All of that."

"I think that was bred out of the Portis gene pool," Viv said. "Miserable family, the lot of them."

"And if Piper is willing to marry him for his ancestry and overlook his abhorrent personality, then she deserves him," Andre said.

"Agreed," I said. "But maybe the castle ghost will stop the wedding and save her."

"Ghost?" Viv asked at the same time Andre said, "What ghost?"

"The ghost of the McKenna bride," I said. "The castle

caretaker Archie Carlton told Harry and me that they get ghost hunters here all the time, looking for her."

"Why is she here?" Andre asked. He skipped over the finger sandwiches and went right for the petit fours. "Is she an angry ghost?"

"He didn't say," I said. "We didn't have much time to talk since he was so annoyed and all."

"How did she die?" Viv asked. "That's the key."

"Apparently, she died right before her wedding, but I don't know the specifics," I said.

"Hmm," Viv said. She lifted her cup and sipped her tea. "Unfinished business, clearly, I can see why she feels the need to haunt the place."

Andre glanced around the room. "Did he say where she likes to do her haunting?"

"No." I studied him. "Do not tell me that you're afraid of the ghost of the McKenna bride. You're the one who told me to expect a ghost in the castle."

"Yes, but that was just in theory and before we got here," he said. He took another petit four. "I wish Nick was here."

"And Alistair," Viv said. This statement was surprising because Viv had been keeping her new relationship with our friend Alistair Turner very private.

"And Harry," I said. "Everything seems so much more reasonable when he's around."

They both nodded and I knew they were thinking the same thing about their partners, although of the three I didn't think Nick was really that much of a stabilizing influence.

There was a knock on the door and then it was flung open. Piper stood there with her hands on her hips, looking very much like the queen of the castle.

"Viv, I need you," she said.

No hi, or how are you, or other nicety.

"I'm not joining your hen party, Piper," Viv said. She popped a tiny curry chicken sandwich into her mouth and chewed.

"It's not about that," Piper said. She tossed her long dark hair over her shoulder. "It's the bridesmaids and tonight's dinner. They're a mess. I mean, how hard is it to pack for a formal dinner? I need you to come and organize their outfits."

"Me?" Viv asked. "I'm a milliner."

"Yes, but you have exquisite taste and they'll listen to you," Piper said.

Viv preened just a little and Andre and I exchanged a look. Piper definitely had Viv's number.

"I suppose I could stop by," Viv said.

"You're a lifesaver," Piper said. She turned and walked back to the door, where she paused. After a beat, she turned around and said, "Was Dooney in here earlier?"

Andre and I both went still. Piper's voice had a calm to it that was like a sheet of ice just before it cracks.

"Yes," Viv said. "He came by to say hi."

"Hi?" Piper asked. She sounded doubtful.

I started to sweat. Had Dooney told her that he thought Viv fancied him? Is that why Piper looked so coldly furious?

74

"Dooney and I went to school together, you know," Andre said.

Piper did a slow pivot in his direction. "I didn't know that. He never mentioned it."

"Oh, it must have slipped his mind," Andre said. "Lots for us to catch up on, I expect."

Piper's spine visibly relaxed. "Well, small world, I suppose."

"Quite," Andre said.

Piper turned back to Viv. "You'll come soon?"

"As soon as I've finished tea," Viv said. She toasted Piper with her cup.

Piper nodded and closed the door behind her.

As soon as it clicked shut, I glanced at Andre and said, "What if she says something to Dooney about seeing you here and he says he never saw you? She'll know you lied."

Andre waved a dismissive hand. "He won't say anything and she won't ask. They have the sort of relationship where they're both horribly jealous but also refuse to let the other person see how jealous they are. Honestly, they're like the worst couple on *Love Island*."

Viv, Fee and I were obsessed with that stupid television show, and I had to agree with Andre that Piper and Dooney would have been perfectly cast.

Viv laughed and said, "Now how am I going to look at them without picturing them on the show? They are ridiculous."

She brushed the crumbs off her fingers and downed her tea. She glanced at me and said, "Are you ready?"

"Me?"

"I'm not going over there alone," she said. "You're the one who wanted to be the milliners to the castle wedding. Whatever fashion emergency is happening, you're helping."

I blew out a breath and sagged against my seat. "All right, fine."

Andre picked up the teapot and warmed up his cup with a refill. He grinned at us and said, "Have fun. Don't worry about me. I'll just take a nap before dinner."

I rose from my seat. "Great idea. Let us know if the ghost comes around."

His smile vanished and he frowned at me. "That was mean."

"Sorry," I said. "I don't want to leave you, but bridesmaids."

He nodded. "Understood."

"Come on, Scarlett," Viv said. "We have to get back here in time to dress for dinner ourselves."

I hurried across the room and fell into step beside her. Out in the corridor, I asked, "Do you even know where we're going?"

"Yes, I passed Piper on the way to our suite," Viv said. "They're in the next corridor."

The rich carpet beneath our feet cushioned our steps. The sconces along the wall emitted a soft light that added to the luxurious feeling of the place. We turned onto the landing, and I glanced down at the great room below. It still took my breath away.

Viv didn't pause to take it in, instead she was striding down the next passageway toward the open door. I could hear the sound of raised voices as I hurried to follow her. I caught up to her just as she pushed the door wide and stepped into a sitting room much like ours.

"I will not wear that hideous color," a curvy blonde announced to the room. "It turns my complexion the color of a fish belly."

"Well, I can't fit into it," a petite brunette said. "I know it's not what you want, Trisha, but sometimes that's life."

"I never get what I want! Otherwise I would be the bride, and not a bridesmaid again!" the one called Trisha shrieked. She threw the sallow-colored cloth at the short brunette, smacking her in the face.

Viv turned to me and said, "We should have had cocktails instead of tea."

Agreed.

Chapter 6

"Viv, darling!" Piper strode across the room. "You're just in time to help with our fashion emergency."

The roomful of women all turned to face the door at once. It was in this moment that Viv's celebrity became our biggest asset. No one was going to argue with a woman who had dressed models on the runways of Paris with her own hats.

Standing behind Viv, I took a moment to soak it all in. In addition to Piper, there were seven women in varying states of undress. Judging by the number of hats Viv and Fee had made, it stood to reason that these were Viv's bridesmaids. All seven of them. Whoa. I didn't think I even had seven friends.

"What seems to be the trouble?" Viv asked. She glanced

around the room with her chin tilted up, looking peak fashionista. There were mutters and grumbles but no one seemed to want to speak. Finally, the one called Trisha cracked.

"Piper told us all to wear a shade of gray to dinner tonight," she said. "She didn't care what shade it was, the important part was that it was neutral so that her yellow dress would stand out in the pictures."

Viv nodded, unsurprised. As for me, I had to battle my eyebrows to stay down because they wanted to rise up at this jaw-dropping display of narcissism. I mean, I get that bridesmaids are supposed to adhere to the bride's chosen color palette at the wedding. We'd done enough hats for bridal parties that I grasped that. But to have them dress in similar colors for a dinner two days before the wedding seemed like an overreach.

Personally, I loved the original intent of having bridesmaids. The custom, dating back to ancient Rome, was that the bridesmaids would dress all in white, exactly like the bride. The theory being that the bridesmaids would confuse evil spirits and potential kidnappers from knowing who the real bride was. So they were more like bodyguards than witnesses to the ceremony. How cool was that?

"I'm failing to see the problem," Viv said. She sounded as forbidding as Meryl Streep in *The Devil Wears Prada*. The women collectively looked nervous, well, all except Piper.

"The problem is that Trisha and Sunny packed the wrong color dresses," Piper said. "Mauve and taupe are not gray."

"I look terrible in gray!" Trisha protested.

Piper ignored her and continued. "There were only two dresses in the village that fit my requirements. This one on Sunny." Piper indicated the brunette, who was in a lovely maxi swing dress in a soft pearl gray.

Sunny had her curly light brown hair twisted into a messy bun at the nape of her neck and was wearing a long double strand of pearls that reached down to her waist. She had round eyes, a turned-up button of a nose and a rosebud mouth. She was also gently rounded, so anything clingy was out of the question.

"And the problem?" Viv asked. She yawned gently, patting her lips. It was a signal that she was running out of patience.

"Sunny has gained some weight—" Piper began but Trisha interrupted.

"Some weight? She's gained a stone!"

I glanced at Sunny. She was turning a scorching shade of hot pink, and I immediately felt sorry for her. Why were some women so nasty to other women? Was there some constant competition to be the prettiest of which I was unaware? Give me a group of overweight, unfashionable, bighearted, funny girls any day over these half-starved, haute couture–wearing, mean, miserable women.

"Only one of the two dresses fits Sunny, so the other one has to be worn by Trisha."

Sunny held up the dress that Trisha had flung at her. The cut was very formfitting, which Trisha, who was skeletally thin, could carry off, but the color did resemble that of a shroud. There was no way to make it pretty.

"I would rather die!" Trisha announced in the most dramatic tone I'd ever heard.

"Show me your other clothes," Viv said.

It was not a tone you argued with. Trisha opened her mouth and then closed it. She led Viv to a standing rack of clothes at the far end of the room. She held her arms out, gesturing to the section that was hers. Viv started sliding the clothes across the rack.

"No, no, no, no." She huffed in frustration.

Then she moved onto the other items, the ones that didn't belong to Trisha. No one said a word but I saw the other bridesmaids shifting on their feet as if they wanted to protest but they didn't dare.

I moved to stand beside Sunny, who was looking particularly miserable, as if this was all her fault.

"Are you all right?" I asked.

She glanced at me with large, sad eyes. It reminded me of Bella when she was being supercute, and I felt my heart go smoosh.

"Yeah sure," she said. "Totally fine." She seemed to shrink into herself a bit as if she didn't want to be noticed.

"Good," I whispered in a low voice only she could hear. "You look terrific in that dress and it never would have suited that one." I gestured at Trisha. "She's too scrawny."

A small smile curved Sunny's lips and she looked pleased. "Thank you."

I nodded and turned back, noticing that Piper was watching me with a curious expression. I pretended not to be aware and focused on Viv. The room was quiet, the tension palpable. The only sound was Viv sliding hangers across the rod, sifting through clothes until she said, "Aha!"

She spun around with a long crocheted vest in her hands in a shade of charcoal gray with crystals worked into the threads making it sparkle in the light. She draped it over Trisha's shoulder with a firm pat.

"Wear that over the dress with some black ballet flats," she said. "You'll look amazing."

She turned away and strode across the room, slipping her arm through mine and pulling me with her. I waved to Sunny, who waved back. Piper hurried to catch up to us.

"Thank you so much, Viv," she cried. "You're a miracle worker."

Viv nodded, knowing quite well that she was. "I'm still not coming to your hen."

"But, Viv," Piper started to protest.

"No." And that was that. Viv ushered us through the door and down the hallway.

"That was impressive," I said as we walked.

"No, it wasn't," she argued. "Anyone could have solved that problem if the women had just offered to share their wardrobes. Instead, they had to call me in to terrorize them into doing it. Ridiculous."

She wasn't wrong.

"I wonder who the vest belonged to," I said.

"I suspect it was the woman who looked slightly ill when I handed it to Trisha," Viv said. "I don't blame her, Trisha is vile."

"She was very mean to Sunny," I said. "A bit of a bully, in fact."

"More than a bit," Viv said. "Going after a woman's weight is unnecessarily vicious. As if we aren't all hounded enough by society's ridiculous expectation that we stay thin and pretty until we die. To heck with that, let's go have some more petit fours."

I laughed. I did adore my cousin and her sense of self. We turned down the passageway that led to our rooms.

"What's the most colorful thing in your suitcase?" Viv asked.

"I have my floral cocktail dress," I said.

"The Jenny Packham with the bright blue morning glory flowers around the hem that wind up across the bodice to the shoulder?"

"That's the one," I said. "I didn't realize drab was the go-to color scheme for the weekend."

Viv laughed. "Piper really hates her bridesmaids. Let's make certain we're not confused with them. You wear the Packham and I have an exotic orange and pink number by Kim Jones that I'm going to wear with a matching hat. I packed one to match your outfit, too."

"Of course you did." I grinned. I wasn't at all surprised that Viv had guessed which dress I was wearing and packed a hat to match. It was my favorite and she knew it. "Piper is not going to be happy with us stealing her limelight."

"Nonsense, we're not stealing anything," Viv said. "We're simply marketing the business."

Right.

* * *

"You two look like exotic birds that took flight in Bermuda and landed here," Andre said. He was in his standard black suit with a black shirt and a bold burgundy tie. His earrings winked in the soft light of the wall sconces as he escorted me and Viv down to one of the larger dining rooms for dinner.

"I think I'd like to be an exotic bird," Viv said. "One with very long curly feathers, naturally."

She gestured to the tiny pillbox hat on her head, which sported one long orange feather that curled around the back. She looked like she belonged in a castle.

I, too, was wearing a hat, the one Viv had packed for me. It was a small confection, round like a cap, embellished with a band of seed pearls all around its edges. It had a puff of blue organza in the center, shaped like a morning glory, which I loved because it added two inches to my height. I wasn't short but I wasn't tall either, so I liked the boost.

We followed the sounds of conversation and arrived at the doors to the dining room at the same time as several other guests. I was relieved to see that they were dressed in suits and cocktail-type dresses. I'd had a brief anxiety spike that this formal dinner meant tuxedos and floor-length gowns, like what the bridesmaids were wearing, and that we'd be outcasts for being underdressed.

Viv had assured me they would never toss us out, but I didn't have her credentials. She had no idea what it was like to be considered expendable.

A hostess greeted us at the door and when we told her our names, she escorted us through the white-cloth-draped tables to the far side of the room. I wondered briefly if we were considered the help and would be served outside, but no.

The balcony doors were open, and I saw the brides-maids gathered around Piper while a bunch of men swarmed Dooney. It seemed all of the weekend guests were in attendance, enjoying the evening air under heat lamps while sipping predinner cocktails.

My stomach gave a lurch of disappointment. Tea felt like ages ago and I was starving. Andre went to fetch us some wine while Viv and I stood apart from the throng. I scanned the crowd and saw Trisha, looking wonderful in her long vest over the unfortunate dress Piper had chosen. Sunny, too, was there looking charming. As I watched, Trisha strode by Sunny and leaned in close to say some-thing. Whatever it was, Sunny paled and then fled the veranda, running right past me and Viv on her way inside.

Viv and I exchanged a look and I knew she hadn't missed Trisha's lean in either.

"Bully." She shook her head.

I thought about following Sunny, but what could I say? Viv had designed hats for enough weddings that I was very aware that these events brought out the worst in some people. I felt fortunate that no matter what venue Harry and I chose for our wedding, none of our people would behave badly at the celebration. At the moment, that felt like such a gift.

"No, no, no." Dooney's voice crested over the sound of

the guests. He was standing at the bar, his arm draped over the shoulders of a man who looked like a fair-haired version of himself. "That bottle of Macallan whiskey is solely for my best mate Quentin and me." He pointed at the bartender. "Understood?"

"Yes, sir, of course." The bartender glanced apologetically at the guest in front of him and removed the glass of amber liquid he'd set down before him.

Dooney reached for it and said, "Let's not let it go to waste." He signaled for the bartender to pour Quentin a whiskey as well, but his friend waved him off.

"Let me finish my vodka tonic first and I'll double back for the Macallan," Quentin said. Dooney looked like he would argue but Quentin said, "The night is young."

Dooney laughed and clapped him on the back. Dooney and his best man, Quentin, were a good-looking pair. Both were tall and slender, wearing well-fitted suits with their hair styled just so. Truly, they looked like models in a men's fashion magazine, and they maneuvered their way around the veranda as if they owned it.

Andre arrived shortly after with white wine for us and a red for himself.

"Cheers." Andre held up his glass.

We tapped our glasses against his and took a restorative sip. He turned to stand beside me and said, "Sorry for the delay. I had to wait for Dooney to depart from the bar."

"He was being obnoxious," I said. "We could hear him all the way over here."

"He looks worse for the wear already," Andre said. "I

have no idea how he's going to get through two more days of this without doing something utterly reprehensible."

"He's clearly already spending the money he plans to marry into," I said. Even from over here, I could see that bottle of Macallan was the good stuff—the several-thousand-pounds-per-bottle type of good stuff.

Dooney was now standing in a circle with his best man and ushers. He was sipping his drink and staring at Piper, the woman who would shortly become his wife. He didn't look like an adoring groom, rather he looked annoyed, as if her very presence grated on his last nerve.

"Did I miss anything over here?" Andre asked.

"Nothing huge," I said. "The bride hasn't slapped the groom or anything."

"Shame."

Viv laughed but then grew serious. She glanced around the veranda and said, "There is a strange tension in the air, do you feel it?"

Andre glanced around. He sounded mildly panicked when he asked, "The ghost? Do you mean the ghost?"

"No," she said. "There just seems to be a divisiveness. Look to the left. See the older couple? He's in the boring suit. She's in the purple sheath with the big gold statement piece around her neck."

"The one that looks like something Wilma Flintstone would wear?" I asked. They both looked at me. "What? It does."

"They're Dooney's parents. Sirus and Davina Portis, very old family line but utterly broke. Destitute, even. Apparently, Sirus has a gambling problem and a stable of mistresses."

"Ew," I said. "That does explain a lot about Dooney."

"And over on the other side of the veranda." Viv tipped her head in that direction and her orange feather bobbed like a pointer. "See the older gentleman, also in a boring suit, and the woman in the flashy silver pantsuit beside him?"

"Hard to miss," Andre said.

"Those are Piper's parents—the Mays, Rita and Matthew," Viv said. "He's a banker by trade and she's an investment broker who was smart enough to build a portfolio with the right tech companies at the right time. They are loaded, more than loaded—if they bought themselves a country of their own, they'd still never be able to spend all of their money."

"Impressive," I said. I glanced back at Sirus and Davina. They looked as if they were in agony but trying to soldier on. Their forced smiles were so brittle I was surprised their faces didn't shatter under the strain. "But not to their daughter's future in-laws, I'm guessing."

"The Portis family has no choice," Viv said. "Dooney either marries into a lot of money or they lose everything, the mansion in London, the country house, the villa in Tuscany, and that's just the properties."

"This is so very nineteenth century," Andre said. "The same as when rich industrialist American families brought their wealthy daughters over to England to bag a bloke with a title."

"As much as things change, they stay the same," Viv said.

"Are both Dooney and Piper aware that they're a money match?" I asked. It seemed so cold and calculated. It made me sad.

"Piper was sent to all the elite schools to meet the proper men so that she could bring the title and connections her parents so desperately crave into the family," Viv said. "At least, that's what it sounded like when she told me her story back when we were all running around London in our midtwenties. She was very specifically networking for a title, which was why she didn't pursue Harrison for very long. He lacked the noble polish she needed to acquire."

"Well, thank goodness for that," I said. I couldn't imagine Harry married to her. He'd be miserable.

We watched as Rita and Matthew worked their way across the room to Sirus and Davina. I watched as Davina saw them coming and closed her eyes as if pained that she was going to have to converse with them.

"This is a conundrum," Andre said.

"In what way?" Viv asked. She sipped her wine and looked at him.

"Well, I'm just not sure which couple I dislike more," he said. "The old money snobs or the grasping newly rich."

"Why do we have to choose?" I asked. I scanned the veranda, looking for the bride and groom. I wondered if they saw their parents heading toward each other like a cruise ship and an iceberg, or maybe that was just me.

Rita made the first move. She tossed her long dark hair, so like Piper's, and leaned in with her arms wide. Davina stiffened once her personal bubble was breached, and the greeting hit a solid ten out of ten on the awkward scale.

It felt as if the entire veranda had gone silent and was watching. I saw Sirus lean over and hiss in Davina's ear. She cast him a look of pure loathing and then stepped forward, her smile as fake as her tan as she flapped around Rita in an air hug before quickly stepping back.

Sirus and Matthew shook hands, resignation slumping both of their shoulders. They didn't meet each other's eyes. The greeting seemed begrudging and was ended as quickly as possible.

I thought about Harry's parents and my parents. They'd met shortly after our engagement when my parents came to London for a visit. I'd been nervous, which was ridiculous, as they got on like long-lost friends to the point where our moms were now in an online book club together and our dads texted each other truly awful dad jokes that they thought were hilarious. Perhaps it helped that my mother was British, but I think it would have worked out that way anyway.

When there is no vast fortune or title or impossible standard to be reached, it was much easier to find common ground in everyday things like your favorite biscuit or vacation spot. Thankfully, they were all in accord about Hobnobs and Aruba.

A laugh from across the veranda brought my attention back to the parents. Rita was telling a story with lots of gestures and a big smile. The men nodded, watching her with an amused detachment while Davina looked slightly ill. Her gaze kept flitting to the right as if she was seeking an escape.

"Where did Dooney go?" I asked. I really felt like this was something he should be dealing with as Piper watched the parents converse from the safety of the circle of her bridesmaids, looking nervous and embarrassed.

We scanned the crowd. There were other guests on the veranda. Viv recognized one as a London-based makeup artist, while others had the look of the Portis family with their distinctive noses, or the May family with their very high foreheads. I wondered briefly how it would work out for any children of Piper and Dooney, especially if they got both the nose and the forehead. Yikes.

"He's over there with Quentin," Viv said. She tipped her head and I followed the direction.

We watched as the two men slipped off the veranda and down the steps. Shortly after, a telltale plume of cigarette smoke rose up from behind the hedges. Like two schoolboys, they'd slipped out of the party to go have a smoke.

I glanced back at Piper. She was glaring at the shrubbery as if she could light it on fire with her fury alone.

"True to form, he's off smoking. I heard she told him he had to quit, but that was years ago. Now he's wandered off, doing whatever he wants and leaving his bride alone," Viv said. "I hope she gets used to that."

It was a depressing observation. I finished my wine. "How much longer do you think it'll be before dinner?"

"At least another twenty minutes," Andre said. He glanced at his watch. "Maybe we should mingle."

Viv looked appalled and I was right there with her, but I also had more pressing matters to attend to. "Sorry, you'll have to make chitchat without me. I'm off to find the loo."

"Leave a trail of bread crumbs," Viv suggested.

"Or just follow the sounds of misery, which is this cocktail hour," Andre said.

I lifted my empty glass to them and headed back into the castle, depositing the glass at the bar on my way.

I stepped into the dining room to find the staff hurriedly prepping the room by filling the water glasses and placing baskets of warm rolls and accompanying butter dishes on the tables. I picked up my pace as I did not want to miss the call to dinner. Out of the dining room, I assumed there would be a bathroom close by. I assumed wrong.

I wandered down the hallway, glancing into each room I passed. Lots of parlors, sitting rooms, a music room, which I had to examine from harp to grand piano to gong—yes, there was an actual gong—but no restroom. I turned around and went back the way I came, choosing a different hallway on my return. No luck. I tapped my foot with impatience. Twenty-plus minutes had definitely passed and I was certain they had begun serving dinner. I looked about for a staff member but they must have all been called to the dining room. There was no one around. I kept going.

Desperate, I tried the first doorknob to my right and

opened it, not expecting it to be a bathroom but checking anyway. It wasn't a bathroom. It was the library, the same one Harrison and I had stumbled upon earlier. I glanced back at the hallway. It did look familiar.

I weighed my need to find a facility against my curiosity about the castle's book collection and, naturally, the books won. I stepped through the door and turned to take in the entire room. The excitement I felt quickly morphed into dread.

Lying in the middle of the floor looking as if he were asleep was Dooney Portis.

Chapter 7

"No, no, no," I muttered to myself. "Not again. Not here. Not now. Not him. Ack!"

I spun around in a useless circle of panic. What was I trying to do? Achieve liftoff? I hurried over to his side. Maybe he was asleep. Maybe he was drunk and passed out. Yes! That had to be it. There was no need to freak out. He seemed the type who would get blasted right before a formal dinner and sleep through the whole thing.

I hitched up my skirt a bit and knelt down beside him. I touched his shoulder. "Hey, wake up."

He didn't wake up.

"Dooney," I said. "Dinner is about to start. You have to be there. Piper is going to be looking for you." I had hoped mentioning his formidable bride-to-be would be enough to bring him out of his sleep coma, but no.

He didn't even twitch. I inhaled through my nose and tried to steady my hands, which were beginning to tremble with a very bad feeling. I needed to get some help. Even if he was just drunk, I couldn't pick him up myself.

My gaze flitted to his face. Gone were the sarcastic sneer and look of disdain. Instead, his features were slack, relaxed even, as though he truly was sleeping. I wished desperately for it to be so, but as I pressed my hand against his face, I was struck by how sunken he looked, as if he'd caved in on himself. He was nonresponsive. No air moved from his nose or mouth. I fell backward and scooted away from him. I'd seen enough. I knew a deceased person when I saw one.

I pushed myself up off the soft carpet and turned toward the door. It was still partly open, and just as I reached it, Archie Carlton appeared. I yelped and put a hand over my chest.

"Mr. Carlton, I'm afraid something terrible has happened," I said.

He looked past me and took in the sight of Dooney on the floor. His face paled beneath his bushy red beard, and his light blue eyes went wide as he muttered, "So, the lass has claimed another."

He stepped forward and checked Dooney's pulse at his wrist. He then put his ear to Dooney's chest. I waited, hoping I'd been wrong. I wasn't. Mr. Carlton stood, turned on his heel and strode from the library. No way was I staying behind. I hurried after him. Once we were outside, he took a key—one of those old-fashioned skeleton-type keys—and turned it in the lock.

"We don't want anyone else stumbling into that room," he said.

"We need to call an ambulance," I said. "And Piper and the Portis family need to be told."

"There's no helping him," Archie said. "I served in the Persian Gulf War. I know a dead man when I see one."

He strode forward, his long legs eating up the hallway as his boot heels thumped against the stone floor. We passed the dining room that was still being set up, and then past several more rooms before he stopped in front of a small office. The castle caretaker didn't bother to knock but pushed open the door and went in.

"Jenkins," he barked. "We have a situation."

The butler, Mr. Jenkins, was standing in front of a small mirror while removing the lint from his black suit with a brush.

"What is it, Carlton?" Jenkins put the brush down and turned away from the mirror.

"It's the curse," Carlton said. "It's happened."

"What's happened?" Jenkins asked.

"The curse of the McKenna bride," Carlton explained. His voice was tight and I realized the burly Scotsman was actually nervous. "The groom is dead."

"What?" Jenkins blinked, uncomprehending.

We needed to get this moving. I stepped forward. "We're mostly certain that he's dead, but if you could call an ambulance, that would be great."

"Ambulance?"

"Aye, the McKenna bride has taken him, but I suppose we'll need medical personnel to confirm," Carlton said.

"What are you talking about?" Jenkins was looking extremely frustrated.

"I found Dooney Portis on the floor of the library a few minutes ago," I said. "He was unconscious. I'm afraid . . ." My voice trailed off. I couldn't say it.

"Dooney Portis is dead?" Jenkins asked. He sounded shocked. "Of the May-Portis wedding, that groom? You're certain?" His body went rigid. I wondered if he was going to have a fit or apoplexy or something even more dramatic that I was unprepared to deal with after finding a dead groom in the library.

"Aye," Archie said. "And the miss here is right. We need an ambulance or an undertaker or something."

"Of course," Jenkins said. He took out his phone and began to scroll through numbers. He strode out the door and down the hallway, clearly expecting us to follow. Carlton shrugged at me and we fell in behind the butler.

I had a brief moment of panic that what I'd seen hadn't been real. That we'd get back to the library and find Dooney drinking a scotch and sitting in front of the fire with a book. Hmm. That seemed unlikely as Dooney hadn't struck me as much of a reader, but still, if he was up and awake, I was going to feel like an idiot. I really hoped I *would* feel like an idiot.

The walk back to the library seemed longer than the walk to find Jenkins had been. I wondered if it was anxiety warping my sense of time. I did not want to be the one to tell the bride her fiancé was dead. Nope. I didn't care how this played out; that was going to be Jenkins's job.

When we reached the library, the door was still locked. Carlton opened it while Jenkins was on his mobile phone requesting an ambulance. We entered the room, and Dooney was exactly where we'd left him. My heart sank. I hadn't realized I'd been clinging so tightly to the hope that I'd been wrong.

Jenkins muttered an oath and hurried across the room, dropping to his knees beside the younger man. He immediately felt for his pulse, checked to see if his chest was rising or falling, and reported the lack of both of these occurrences to the dispatcher on the phone.

Carlton and I stood witness to the scene in front of us. Jenkins shoved his free hand in his hair. I heard him say, "It's no use." He bowed his head.

Feeling faint, I leaned into the caretaker and to my surprise, he put one of his burly arms around my shoulders and gave me a firm squeeze. "It'll be all right, miss."

It wouldn't be, but I appreciated the gesture nonetheless. Jenkins rose slowly to his feet. He continued speaking to the dispatcher and gestured for us to leave the library. Carlton and I were first to step into the hallway, and Jenkins followed. He was about to pull the door shut behind him when Piper appeared.

"Oh, no," I said.

Carlton tried to reach around Jenkins to close the door but to no avail as Piper bore down on us with the fierceness of a Valkyrie.

"Mr. Jenkins, have you seen my intended?" she asked. "Mr. Portis?"

We all froze. Jenkins looked momentarily nonplussed. I couldn't blame him. I had no idea how he was going to break the news to her.

"I'm so sorry, Miss May," he said. His voice was grave.

"Sorry?" she asked. "Whatever for?" She glanced at the three of us and then at the library behind us. I didn't think she could see Dooney, but I supposed it was just a matter of time. "What is going on here?"

Jenkins stood immobile, looking as if he longed to wish the situation away. I understood that, but it wasn't going to happen.

"Piper, about Dooney," I said. She turned to look at me, and her eyes narrowed with suspicion. Both Carlton and Jenkins looked at me in relief. Cowards. "I . . . well . . . I don't know how to say this."

"Just say it," Piper demanded.

"Dooney is dead," I said. I couldn't get clearer than that.

Jenkins heaved a sigh, and I took that to mean he was disappointed at my inability to speak in British understatement. What should I have said? That Dooney was taking a permanent nap?

"That's not funny, Scarlett," Piper snapped.

"No, it isn't," I said. Something in my tone must have gotten through to her.

"I want to see him," she said. "Now."

Jenkins shook his head but I nodded. I would feel the

same if someone said that to me about Harry. We had to show her.

"Mr. Carlton, can you go out to the front to meet the . . . uh . . . people we're expecting and escort them here?" Jenkins asked.

"Of course." Carlton nodded. He took off, looking relieved to be putting distance between himself and the scene that was to come.

"I'm so sorry, Miss May, if you'll follow me," Jenkins said. He pushed the door open and led her into the room.

With a frown, Piper followed him. She stopped as soon as she saw Dooney on the floor. "Dooney!" She turned to look at us. "He must be drunk. He just fell asleep. Right?"

I shook my head.

"I'm sorry, Piper, but Dooney has passed away," I said. It sounded so weird coming out of my mouth.

"No, you're mistaken," she said. "We're getting married in two days. He's just unconscious or something."

"No," Mr. Jenkins said. "Miss Parker is right. We have an ambulance and the police coming, but I'm afraid the ambulance is just a formality. Mr. Portis is deceased."

"No." She shook her head, covered her mouth with her hand and then fainted, crumpling where she stood so fast that Jenkins barely had time to catch her before she hit the carpet. She would have been concussed if he hadn't snatched her up at the last second.

Jenkins lowered her the rest of the way to the ground. We stared at each other. It was a safe bet that neither of us had been in this kind of situation before.

"What do we do?" I asked. I was hoping Jenkins was the sort of unflappable butler who had a plan. He wasn't. He did not.

"I have no idea," he cried. He took a handkerchief out of his inside breast pocket and mopped his forehead. "Do we shut her in here until the constable arrives?"

"We can't shut her in here with the body of her fiancé," I protested. "That's just wrong."

"Fine, you stay with her then," he said.

"What?" I cried. "No! I don't want to stay with her."

"Someone has to," he said. "I need to stand guard outside to make certain no one else comes in here."

Well, he had me there. I admittedly wouldn't be as effective as a guard. Dang it.

"All right, I'll try and rouse her," I said.

Jenkins left the room, shutting the library door behind him with a decisive click. I crouched down next to Piper. What was it they did in all the old novels, pat their hands? I patted her hand. She didn't flicker so much as a false eyelash. Smelling salts? Didn't have any. Cold water poured over her head? Seemed harsh. Also, I didn't have any.

"Piper, it's me, Scarlett, Viv's cousin," I said. "I know you've had a shock, but you need to wake up."

Why? my brain argued. If I were Piper, I'd want to stay unconscious, too.

I glanced around the library to see if there was anything I could use to nudge her back to consciousness. I had no idea how long it would take for help to arrive.

The waist-high bookcases in the center of the library

made it easy to see across the room. I glanced down the rows and saw a swatch of gray fabric behind one of the cases. I was certain it hadn't been there when I found Dooney. I was positive I would have noticed. I slowly rose to my feet and crept toward the bookcase. I knew I recognized the cloth, but from where?

I jumped around the shelf, wobbling a bit on my heels, and there, crouched on the floor, was Sunny in the pearl gray dress that had caused such a to-do between her and Trisha—that's why I recognized it.

"Sunny, what are you doing in here?"

Her face was blotchy and she looked as if she'd been crying. Her voice when she spoke was punctuated with hiccups.

"I—came into the library to gather my thoughts. Then I saw Dooney and rushed to help him, but he"—she hiccuped again—"was—" She sobbed.

"The door was locked," I said. "How did you get in here?"

"There's another entrance," she said.

"The tunnel," I said.

She nodded. "I was outside walking the grounds—then found a door at the far end of the garden. It led here but when I came inside—Dooney—"

"I know, it's awful," I said. "But why are you hiding?"

"I thought—" She paused and took a steadying breath. "I thought it would look bad if I was found with him, and I panicked when I heard the three of you come in."

I nodded. So, she'd come in through the tunnel during the time Archie and I went off to find Jenkins. I was in the unique position to appreciate exactly how freaked out she might have been to find the groom dead in the library.

"Come on," I said. "Let's see if we can help Piper."

Sunny nodded and swiped at her face with her hands. She took the hand I held out, and I pulled her to her feet. Together, we went back to Piper, who was still out cold.

"Help me try to wake her," I said.

"Of course." Sunny knelt on one side while I took the other.

"Piper," I said. I tried to sound as commanding as Viv. "Piper, wake up."

I saw her eyelids flutter.

"She's coming round," Sunny said. She didn't talk to Piper or touch her in any way, leaving it to me. I glanced at Sunny and noticed she was staring at Dooney with an expression I couldn't decipher. If I had to label it, I'd have called it a mixture of stunned disbelief and grief.

"Sunny, help me get her up," I said. Piper's eyes were opening, and I figured we should get her out of there before she remembered everything and became hysterical, for which I really couldn't blame her.

"What happened?" Piper asked. Her voice was faint. "I remember I came into the library—"

"And then you fainted," I said. I figured if we skipped ahead, she might not remember why she'd fainted and we could get her out the door before she spotted Dooney again.

"I did?" she asked. She glanced from me to Sunny. "What are you doing here, Sunny?"

"Oh . . . um . . . I just happened by," she said.

I glanced at her over Piper's head but she didn't meet

my gaze. At that moment, the door to the library was thrust open and several NHS EMTs appeared with Jenkins, followed by two constables. Things were about to get intense.

"What's happening?" Piper asked. "Did you call an ambulance for me? I'm fine."

"It's not for you," Sunny said. Her voice was rough with emotion. Piper watched the men walk right past us to Dooney.

She let out a little scream and covered her mouth with her hand. "I remember! Oh, no! Dooney!"

Her voice was a cry of such utter gut-wrenching loss that I actually flinched. One of the constables came over and helped Piper to her feet.

"Let's get you out of here, ma'am," he said. Piper looked like she'd dig in her heels and resist, but he was able to lead her to the door where Jenkins stood, looking like he was trying to control the situation from afar.

Sunny and I followed Piper and the constable out to the hallway. I had no idea what to say or do. I wanted to get back to Vivian and Andre but I couldn't exactly leave. Carlton was standing outside the door. Though he looked as forbidding as usual, I found comfort in his glowering presence.

"What happened to my fiancé?" Piper asked the constable.

"I don't know, ma'am," he said. "As soon as we have some information, we'll be sure to share it with you. Is there anyone else who should be here? Does he have any family present?"

Piper looked stricken. "His parents. They're probably on their way to the dining room right now."

The constable looked at Jenkins. "Could you bring them here quietly?"

"With the utmost discretion," Jenkins said. He hurried down the hallway, clearly relieved to be doing something.

"I'm going to talk to the medical personnel and my colleagues," the constable said to Piper. He glanced at Sunny and me. "Can you stay with her?"

"Of course," we said together.

"I'll keep an eye on them," Carlton said. "To make sure no one faints and the like."

The constable took in the burly Scot and seemed satisfied. He turned and went back into the library.

"I can't believe this is happening," Piper said. "I think I'm going to be sick."

Just like that, Carlton was thrusting a small rubbish bin at her. She took it and clutched it to her chest. The hallway grew quiet. We could hear the murmur of voices from the library but not what they were saying. Time seemed to be moving backward and I had to force myself to stand still and not pace.

"Where is he?" a voice cried. "Where is my son?"

I glanced up to see Davina Portis striding down the hallway. Her eyes were wide and her nostrils flared. Her husband was hurrying to keep up. When she entered the library, her scream was so anguished it rang in my ears for hours that night.

The pain in her cry was excruciating, the grief of a mother confronting the death of her child. I felt Sunny

106

slide her hand into mine, and I glanced at her. She was pale and shaking and tears were coursing down her cheeks. She was feeling it, too.

Piper, on the other hand, dropped the rubbish bin she'd been holding and strode toward the library. Her expression was fierce.

I had a very bad feeling about this.

Chapter 8

"Get out! Get out! Get out!" Davina shouted from inside the library. As one, Sunny, Carlton and I all flinched.

Moments later, Mr. Portis came out of the library with Piper. His hand was clenched around her elbow, and her shoulder was pushed up against her ear.

"Kindly leave us," he said. Then he let her go and went back into the library.

Piper rubbed her elbow. Tears were coursing down her cheeks.

"Are you all right?" Sunny asked.

Piper looked up and her expression was one of deep fury. "How dare they? Did you see that? He's my husband to be. I should be in there and they just tossed me out like I was nothing."

She wasn't wrong. I found it extremely odd that Mr. and Mrs. Portis had dismissed her from the room. Dooney was her fiancé, and they were to be married in a matter of days. Shouldn't she be with them during this horrific time?

One of the constables came out of the library. He glanced down the hallway as if he was expecting someone. He checked his phone, glanced down the hall again, checked his phone, rinse and repeat, until a person appeared at the end of the corridor.

He was a tall man, with very short gray hair and prominent ears. He looked to be in his late forties although he had the lanky build of a soccer—excuse me, football—player. The constable was clearly relieved to see him. He even let out a small sigh.

"Detective Inspector Stewart," he said. "Thanks for coming out so late. The . . . er . . . situation is in here."

The detective paused and looked at the three of us. "Who are you?"

"I'm Piper May, the deceased's bride-to-be," Piper said. Her voice wobbled a bit on "deceased."

The inspector's gaze never left her face. He had light brown eyes and a beak of a nose, but his strong chin balanced it out. He wasn't good-looking in the classical sense, but he had one of those faces that grows on you in time. After a few years, you'd wonder why you never thought he was handsome before.

"I'm Archie Carlton, castle caretaker," Carlton introduced himself. The detective nodded.

"I'm Sunny Bright," Sunny said. I hadn't caught her surname before and it caught me by surprise. I wasn't alone.

"Really?" the detective asked.

"Yes, really," she said. There was just the faintest bit of testiness in her voice which led me to believe she had to answer for her name a lot. She added, "I'm a bridesmaid."

"And you are?" the detective asked me.

"I'm Scarlett Parker," I said. "Hatmaker—well, I don't really make the hats. That's my cousin Viv, she's around here somewhere, she can vouch for me. Not that I think I need anyone to vouch for me since I didn't do anything wrong." *Hush up*, I chastised myself, *blathering on is not helping you.*

"And why are you here, Scarlett Parker?"

"I was actually looking for a bathroom," I said. "Big as this place is, they really hide the necessaries." This reminded me of how badly I had to go and I hopped from foot to foot.

Detective Stewart looked at Carlton and said, "Maybe you could escort her to the nearest loo?"

"Aye, I can do that," he said.

"Come right back," Detective Stewart said. "I have more questions for all of you."

Sunny let out a low moan that only I could hear. I suspected she was freaking out. I was right there with her. I mean, there was no way that saying you were looking for a bathroom and just happened to stumble upon a dead body didn't sound lame, right?

"This way, miss," Carlton said.

I glanced at Sunny to see if she wanted to come, but Piper said, "She stays with me."

Sunny nodded, signifying that this was okay. Carlton had already started to walk down the hallway. I hurried after him. Tucked into an alcove was the bathroom, with no sign or symbol signifying what it was. I pushed open the door and hurried inside.

I'd been hoping that the facility was closer to the dining room so I could signal Andre and Viv that I was okay. They had to be seated for dinner by now, right? I had no idea if the Portises' departure from the party had informed the rest of the guests that something was amiss. In fact, with both the bride and the groom not at the dinner, weren't people wondering what was happening?

I know I would be. In fact, if I were Viv and Andre, I'd be looking for me. Were they looking for me? I'd bet real money they were. I'd left my handbag with Viv so I couldn't call them or text them or touch up my lipstick—not that I wanted to do that right now.

I made quick work of my business, and then after washing my hands, I hurried outside to find Carlton still waiting for me. I wasn't sure he would. If he hadn't been, I would have tried to find the dining room, despite the detective telling us not to go anywhere.

"I feared you might get lost on your way back," he said.

"I probably would have," I admitted.

He turned back toward the library. I didn't want to go. I didn't want to think about Dooney or Piper or their parents or the colossal nightmare this weekend had become.

I needed to call Harry and see if he could collect us right away. I didn't want to spend another second in this castle of horrors.

When we arrived back at the entrance to the library, Piper and Sunny were still standing outside. Sunny looked sad but Piper appeared shocked, as if she couldn't believe what was happening. I was right there with her.

The doors to the library opened and Sirus and Davina came out. He was holding her up as she sobbed into her hands. Beyond them I could see that the medics had draped a cloth over Dooney, confirming that he was dead.

"What's happening?" Piper asked. Her voice cracked and she tried again with more authority in her voice. "Tell me what's happening!"

Davina's head snapped up. Her tear-soaked face turned a violent shade of red, and she shoved away from her husband and staggered toward Piper. "You!" she shrieked.

Piper backed up.

"You aren't worth the starch in his collar!" she declared. "You're just social-climbing rubbish—"

"Davina!" Sirus snapped. She ignored him.

"Do you want to know what I think?" Davina stalked toward Piper, backing her up against the wall. Piper leaned back, trying to maintain her space, but Davina wasn't having it.

I felt like I should do something, but what? Davina was clearly out of her mind with grief. What could I possibly do to stop her when her own husband just stood there, looking impotent?

"No, what do you think?" Piper asked. Her voice was just above a whisper.

"I think the thought of marrying you, of being stuck with someone so out of his own social class, caused him to die of a heart attack," Davina hissed. "You are so far beneath him and he knew it, but he did it for—"

"Davina, stop it right now!" This time Sirus's voice was a command. Davina didn't care. She turned on him. Her hair was falling around her face; her mascara circled her eyes. She looked like the grief was shredding her from the inside out.

"Stop it?" she spat at her husband. "We wouldn't even be here if it weren't for you and your mismanagement of your inheritance. You speculated and lost and our son, our only child, took it upon himself to marry this—" She waved a dismissive hand at Piper. "This parvenu."

That didn't sound good. I hadn't gotten the warm fuzzies off Davina and Sirus from the moment I laid eyes on them, and I didn't particularly like Piper either, but right now, after that horrible woman said those vicious things, I was 100 percent Team Piper. I wasn't the only one.

"What did you just call my daughter?" We all turned around to see Rita storming down the hallway. Gone was the ingratiating smile. Instead, she looked like she would happily slap Davina across the face.

"It's all right, Mum," Piper said. "Something terrible has happened and Davina is upset."

Rita moved to stand beside Piper. She stared down at Davina. "What could possibly have happened that she would speak to you like that?"

Davina turned away from them as if she couldn't bear to look at the mother and daughter. Piper turned in to her mother's arms and put her head on her shoulder. Then she sobbed.

Carlton cleared his throat and said to Mr. and Mrs. Portis, "You'll be wanting to sit in the drawing room, I expect."

"No, I don't—" Davina argued but Carlton cut her off.

"Follow me." He looked at Sirus expectantly, and Sirus nodded. He took his wife's elbow and they followed Carlton to another room down the hall.

At that moment the detective inspector stepped out of the library. He saw Carlton leading Sirus and Davina away, and he glanced at Rita and Piper.

"How are you, miss?" he asked. His voice was kind. I didn't know if he had heard what Davina had unleashed on Piper, but I suspected he might have.

"Who are you?" Rita asked. "What is this all about?"

Piper stepped back. Her voice was small and she sobbed when she said, "It's Dooney, Mum. He's . . . he's . . . dead."

Rita gasped. She covered her mouth with her hand. "What? How? Are you—"

"Sure?" Piper asked. She glanced at the detective. He nodded and she turned back to her mother. "Yes, I'm sure."

Rita put her hand over her chest and sagged into the wall. "I can't . . . I don't understand." She was very pale, and I was afraid she might faint like Piper had.

"Is there something I can get for you?" I asked.

Rita looked at me without really seeing me. "My husband. I need my husband."

I looked at the detective. He nodded. "Do not speak to anyone else. Do not tell anyone else what is happening. Am I clear?"

"Yes." I glanced at Sunny to see if she wanted to come with me but she was staring at the floor looking morose. Maybe it was better if she stayed away from the crowd for now. "I'll be right back."

I turned and hurried down the hallway. No, I had no idea where the dining room and veranda were, but I was hoping that the guests would be making enough noise that I could follow the sound. I turned left at a suit of arms that I remembered, then I went straight and ended up at a dead end, where I saw a game room of sorts, with a big billiards table. I turned, went back the way I came and took the only other passageway available.

I was doubting myself, when I heard the faint sound of chatter and laughter. Excellent. I was so close. I knew I wasn't supposed to stop and talk to anyone else, but if I saw Viv and Andre, there was no way I couldn't tell them what was happening.

The guests had left the veranda and were now in the dining room. I glanced around until I saw Mr. May standing beside his table, looking concerned as he watched the doors. I wondered if he sensed something was amiss.

I hurried across the room toward him. I had a sudden pang of anxiety at the thought that we'd get lost as I tried to lead him to the library. I pushed it aside. I'd figure it out. I was halfway across the room when Viv appeared in front of me.

"Scarlett, where have you been?" Viv cried. "Andre was convinced you'd fallen in the moat and drowned."

"There is no moat," I said.

"Details." She waved her hand at me. "Aren't you starving? I think they're about to start serving. You didn't happen to see Piper in the loo, did you? Because she's disappeared, too, and I doubt we'll be able to start without her. Dooney has been missing even longer than her. I wonder if they're having a spat. You don't think they'd call off the wedding, do you?"

We were in the middle of the dining room, surrounded by people. What was I supposed to say? I couldn't say anything without giving away what was happening.

"I can't talk right now," I said. "I need to fetch Mr. May. His wife needs him."

"Oh, no," Viv cried. "We're never going to eat, are we?"

"I can't answer that," I said. "I can't answer anything, but I'm guessing no."

I was starting to panic. Viv narrowed her eyes at me. "You know something."

"No, I don't," I lied.

Andre appeared behind Viv. "Scarlett, finally, we were getting worried."

"No need," I said. "I just have to take care of one little thing and I'll be right back."

Before I could get caught in another conversation, I spun away from them and hurried to Mr. May.

"Hi," I said. "Mrs. May sent me to get you."

"Get me?" he asked. He frowned, looking annoyed. I remembered he was a banker. He probably didn't like that things were off schedule. Well, he was about to get a lot more uncomfortable.

"There's been a bit of an incident," I said. Clearly, I'd been in London too long as I was beginning to master the British art of understatement. Something in my tone must have given it away, because he nodded.

"Is Rita all right?" he asked.

"Yes, she's fine," I said. I began to walk to the exit. "As is Piper, but they could use your assistance."

He followed without question. Once we made it out into the hallway, I tried to retrace my steps.

"Forgive me, I don't remember your name," he said.

"I'm Scarlett Parker," I said. "I work at the millinery that made the bridesmaid hats for the ceremony."

"Oh, yes, of course," he said. "Damned expensive those hats."

I almost laughed at his candor but this was no time for amusement. I just wanted to deliver him as swiftly as possible and then go hide in my room and drink an entire bottle of wine.

We hurried down the hallway. I knew I had a turn to make and—yes!—I went in the right direction. When we arrived at our destination, no one was in the hallway. I could see people through the open door of the library, but Dooney's body was no longer there. I had no idea if the medics or a coroner had taken him away.

I knew that Piper and her mother were likely in another sitting room or salon in the corridor. I saw a door that was partly open and peeked inside to find Carlton and Sunny.

"Are the Mays next door?" I asked.

"Across the hall in the green room," he said.

I nodded my thanks. I don't know if Mr. May felt the sudden shift in the atmosphere but he became very quiet. I couldn't blame him. The tension felt as heavy as a cement slab lying on my chest.

We crossed the hall quickly. I could hear the sound of Mrs. Portis sobbing in a room down the hall. Judging by the way Mr. May's shoulders stiffened, he could hear it, too. I knocked on the door and then turned the knob and pushed the door open.

The green room was aptly named with green carpet, lighter green walls and green-and-cream-brocade upholstery on the heavy wood furniture. Piper and her mother were seated together on a divan. Rita had her arm around Piper, who was sobbing into her mother's shoulder.

"Rita, Piper, my dears," Mr. May cried. "Whatever is the matter?"

"Oh, Daddy," Piper sobbed. "They think I killed him."

Chapter 9

"What are you talking about?" Mr. May asked as he rushed over to his wife and daughter. He took Piper's hands in his. "Killed whom?"

"Dooney," Piper sobbed.

"I don't understand." Matthew May rocked back on his heels.

Rita rose from her seat. She smoothed her pantsuit and explained, "Dooney was found dead in the library." Then she gestured to me and said, "By her."

Mr. May glanced back at me. "You might have mentioned this on the walk over."

"Sorry," I said. "I wasn't sure how to work it into the conversation, and I thought it would be better for you to hear it from your wife and daughter."

He nodded. "I'd have done the same, I suppose." He turned back to Piper. "Why would they think you killed him? How did he die?"

"We don't know yet," Rita said. "The detective is speaking with his parents and he said he'd come talk to us next."

"His parents?" Matthew May scoffed. "Those insufferable toffs."

I suspected this was the opposite slam to "parvenu." I began to ease my way to the door. This was clearly time for the family to be alone together, and the least I could do was give them some privacy.

The open door was right behind me. All I needed to do was take one more step, but before I could, a hand grabbed my arm and I was yanked into the hallway, the door closing after me. I yelped but if the Mays heard me, they didn't care. I expected to see the detective or a constable standing there holding my elbow, but instead it was Viv with Andre beside her.

"What are you two doing here?" I cried. "You're going to get me in trouble."

"What are we doing here?" Viv huffed. "You're the one who disappeared. What's going on? They started serving dinner but they also placed waitstaff at the doors and told us we couldn't leave the dining room until further notice."

"How did you two get out?"

"Kitchen," Andre said. "They didn't have anyone stationed by the kitchen."

"Clever." I glanced up and down the hallway, waiting

for a constable to swoop down on us and chastise me for having people here. "Come on," I said. I led them into the room where Sunny and Carlton were waiting.

They both looked up when we entered. Archie's eyebrows rose, and Sunny gave Viv a watery smile. They were seated in chairs in front of the fireplace, which was lit and giving off a nice warmth in the chill of the late-spring evening. I moved to stand in front of it as the cold seemed to have crept into my bones. I hugged my arms around my middle and tried to gather my thoughts.

"You remember Sunny," I said. "And this is the castle caretaker, Archie Carlton."

"Hi, Sunny," Viv said. She smiled at Archie. "Pleasure to meet you, Mr. Carlton."

"Call me Archie." As most men do, he looked dazzled by Viv as she turned her charm up to medium. If she pushed it to high, the poor man would probably keel over.

"Nice to meet you," Andre said. He nodded at both of them.

"This is my cousin, Vivian Tremont, and our friend, Andre Eisel, who is also the wedding photographer," I said.

"Don't think they'll be needing that service any longer," Archie said. Sunny sobbed and he looked contrite. "Sorry, miss."

"No, it's fine," she said. "I'm just still in shock."

Viv sat on the love seat and Andre sat beside her. "All right, I feel as if I'm going mad. What's happened?"

"I—" I began but I was interrupted by the detective inspector, who had obviously been listening at the door.

"There's been an incident," Detective Inspector Stewart said. "Might I ask what you two are doing here, Ms. Tremont, when I am certain I left explicit instructions that no one should leave the dining room?"

"Scarlett is my cousin," Viv said. "She went to use the loo ages ago and never came back. Naturally, we came looking for her. We were terrified she was lost. Now, since we are here, kindly tell us, sir, what is happening so that we can be of service instead of being a nuisance."

She'd jacked up the charm meter to high. Detective Stewart studied her for a moment and then a ghost of a smile curved his mouth, but it quickly vanished, and he tugged on the tip of one of his large ears while he schooled his features into a stern expression.

"Approximately thirty-seven minutes ago, Dooney Portis was found in the library, deceased," he said.

Viv gasped. Andre blanched. Sunny sobbed even harder. I twisted my fingers together, and Archie said, "The ghost claims another."

"What ghost?" Sunny asked. She looked at me. "There's a ghost?"

I shrugged.

"The McKenna bride," Archie said. "She died tragically before her own wedding, and now weddings in Waverly Castle are cursed. It's said she haunts the castle to this day, ruining the nuptials of any who dare to wed here."

To his credit, the detective ignored Archie and continued, "We don't know the cause of death at this time, but his parents have informed us that he was in excellent health. We will be conducting a full investigation and would appreciate everyone's cooperation."

"Of course," Viv said. "Anything to help. Do you want us to give you our contact information in London?"

"Oh, you're not going to London," he said.

"Not tonight, obviously," she said. "But first thing in the morning since there won't be a wedding."

"I don't think you understand, Ms. Tremont," he said. "Until we know whether we're dealing with a murder, no one who was here during the time of Mr. Portis's death will be leaving the castle until our investigation is completed."

"They can't keep us here indefinitely, can they?" Andre asked.

"No," Viv said. She sounded more confident than I felt. "Overnight at best."

We were back in the dining room with all of the other guests. We'd missed dinner but had managed to arrive in time for trifle and coffee. I fully intended to hit the kitchen for a sandwich before bed. I wish I could say finding the groom deceased caused me to lose my appetite, but no. If anything, I needed comfort food more than ever.

There was a low rumble reverberating around the room. I suspected the rumors about where the bride and groom and their parents were had started to infiltrate the gathering. Not a big surprise, given that they all had missed dinner. I wondered how everyone was going to take the announcement of Dooney's passing. Would they announce it? I supposed they had to.

Detective Inspector Stewart had interviewed me before letting us return to the dining room. I didn't have much to tell him. I'd been looking for a loo and found Dooney instead. It was a terrible story. Whatever the detective thought about it, he kept to himself. He called Archie in after me, and then Sunny.

She came out of the room, obviously distraught, and Viv and I tried to comfort her, but it was no use. I wondered if I had responded to my first dead body with this much upset. I thought back to my first few days in London where I had the misfortune of finding one of our clients murdered, wearing only the hat that Viv had made for her. Yeah, I was definitely as upset as Sunny, but unlike Sunny, I hadn't known the victim very well.

"Do you think Sunny will be all right?" I asked Viv, who was sitting on my left.

We were sharing a table with some of the May cousins down from Yorkshire. They were not a particularly chatty group, and after the initial introductions, they ignored the three of us, which was fine with me, as I wasn't feeling very social at the moment.

"I don't know," Viv said. "She doesn't seem to have a rapport with the other girls. She didn't go to university with Piper and she's not a childhood friend. Honestly, I can't figure out why Piper put her in the wedding."

I followed her gaze to the table where the bridesmaids sat. Sunny did look ostracized from the group. I wondered if that was Trisha's doing. Maybe she was still mad about the dress and punishing Sunny by turning the others against her. When everyone found out what was happening and that Sunny had stumbled upon Dooney's body in the library, I imagined their curiosity would get the better of them and they'd be more inclusive with her. People could be peculiar like that.

Detective Inspector Stewart entered the dining room. Sirus and Davina Portis weren't with him but Matthew and Rita May were, as was Piper. Their faces were somber. I had no idea what to expect, and put down my fork and picked up my coffee cup. The delicate china felt fragile in my fingers. I took a restorative sip. It helped a little.

There was a microphone at the head table. Obviously, speeches had been planned. I wondered what Dooney would have said tonight and on his wedding day to the guests who had come from far away to attend this monster wedding. We were just the VIPs, who got to spend the weekend here. Andre had told me that the expected attendance on the day of the wedding was over four hundred.

Detective Inspector Stewart picked up the microphone. One of the castle employees paused beside him and helped him turn it on. I expected the microphone to squeal with feedback like it always does in the movies when someone is about to make a critical speech, but it didn't.

"Good evening, ladies and gentlemen," he said. He cleared his throat. "I'm Detective Inspector Stewart."

This announcement caused the room to go quiet as the guests stilled. Forks stopped in midair. Coffee cups were gently put back on their saucers. Lips were patted with napkins. Everyone gave the detective their full attention.

Even knowing what he was about to tell them, I felt the same sense that something big was happening.

"It is with heartfelt sympathy that I must share some tragic news," he said. His voice was low and deep, soothing but somber. "It appears that Dooney Portis passed away this evening."

"What?" Quentin cried. He looked stunned. As Quentin was his best man, I imagined it had to be more than a little shocking to learn that his best mate, whom he'd just been having a cigarette with, was dead. "Is this a joke?"

"No," Piper cried. She met Quentin's gaze. "It's true."

Stunned silence met his words and then, as the news sank in, gasps and cries of disbelief filled the air. Piper put a hand over her face and sobbed. Her parents immediately hugged her, one on each side.

"How?" Quentin asked. "I don't understand."

"I'm sorry, at this time we're not at liberty to discuss the cause of death, but we will be investigating," Detective Stewart said.

I watched as the rest of the guests processed the news. Dooney Portis was dead. There would be no wedding. There would be an investigation because the police didn't know how he died. It took about seven seconds before a voice spoke over the shocked murmurs and mutterings.

"Was he murdered?" a woman at another table asked.

I saw Rita glare at the woman over Piper's head. The woman was sitting at one of the tables reserved for the Portis family. Interesting.

"Again, I can't answer any questions at this time," Detective Inspector Stewart said. "You will all be questioned over the next few days as we try to determine the cause of death. We will, of course, keep the families posted on our findings."

The rumble started up again. This time there was more outrage and indignation.

"Are you saying that you're keeping us all here for a few days?" a man at another table demanded.

"Correct," Detective Inspector Stewart said. "My team will be stationed all over the castle. I suggest that once dinner is finished, you all retire to your rooms. There will be a nightly curfew of ten o'clock while the investigation is underway."

Viv slowly turned her face toward me. "A weekend in a castle, you said. It'll be fun, you said."

I winced. "Sorry."

"Not nearly as sorry as I am," she said. She tossed her napkin onto the table and rose to her feet. "I'm going to bed."

Andre and I rose, too. "Wait for us. You can't wander around the castle alone."

"Of course I can," Viv said. "Nothing's going to happen to me."

"You don't know that," I said. "What if Dooney was just a victim of convenience? What if there is a serial killer at this wedding and they murder anyone they find alone?"

"Scarlett," Viv scolded. "Rein in your imagination, or else there will be no more mystery shows for you."

I felt someone staring at me and glanced over to see the May cousins all watching me with their eyes wide and their mouths open. They looked petrified.

"Oh, I'm not saying there is a serial killer," I said. "Just that, you know, you should be careful."

They huddled together, not even acknowledging me. Okay then.

Viv was walking away. Andre and I fell into step behind her.

"Do you believe what the caretaker Archie said?" Andre asked.

"Which thing that Archie said?" I asked.

"That the murderer is the ghost?" he asked.

"Why would a ghost want to kill Dooney Portis?" I asked.

"Because he was . . . not a good person," he said.

"Piper isn't an especially good person either," I said. "If that was the criteria, wouldn't the ghost have gone after her, too?"

"It only takes one death to stop a wedding," Andre said. "Maybe Dooney was a more convenient target."

"I don't know," I said. "I don't even know if I believe in ghosts. I certainly don't know if one could kill a person. I mean, they don't have the physical means to murder, so how could they cause a death? Scare someone into a heart attack?"

"That's it. I'm sleeping on the couch in your sitting room," he said. "I absolutely can't sleep alone in my room. I'll die of fright."

"We've got you," I said. "Right, Viv?"

"You may sleep wherever you want, Andre," she said. "Our suite is your suite."

"Thank you," he said. "I'll get my things and be right over."

Viv and I entered our suite while Andre went on to his own. I didn't lock the door, knowing that he would return shortly. I stared at the divan. It seemed short for Andre, and I realized I'd better take it and give him my bed. Yes, because I am an awesome friend like that.

Viv stomped across the sitting room to her room. I could tell by her posture, back straight and chin jutting out, that she was mad. Usually when Viv was in a mood, I avoided her and let her cool down. But we were stuck here, so I figured it would be better to let her vent.

"You're upset," I said.

"Upset? Me? Whyever would I be upset?" she asked. Her voice was full of that annoying exaggeration people do when they're really mad but not quite to the throwing-things stage.

"Wild guess here," I said. "It's because we're stuck here for a few days."

"By George, I think you've got it."

"Sarcasm doesn't become you, Viv," I said. I plopped down on the divan. It was surprisingly comfy. "Besides, why are you so angry? We'd have been here for a few days for the wedding anyway. Now we're just here for a police investigation."

"If you remember right, I didn't want to do this wedding to begin with," she said. "This job was your idea because you wanted a weekend in the country in a castle. Well, now we're trapped."

"And?" I asked. I still didn't see a major difference between being here for the wedding and being here for the investigation, although I understood that it was obviously a much less happy circumstance.

"You promised me we'd go to the village and meet Dominick Falco, which is the only reason I even agreed to this fiasco, and now we can't even do that."

She crossed the room to the stack of seven hatboxes that contained the bridesmaids' wedding hats. She lifted the lid off one and moved the tissue paper aside to stare down at one of the blush-colored fascinators she and Fee had created.

She lifted the delicate hat out of the box. It was a puff of pale pink feathers fastened onto a matching satin cap that was trimmed with seed pearls and a jaunty bow. The fascinators were an exact match for the dresses and would have looked stunning on the bridesmaids.

"Maybe we can sell them in the shop?" I suggested. "Or save them for another wedding? Blush is very popular these days."

Viv heaved a sigh and nestled the hat back into its tissue. "Maybe, but I still can't believe this is happening. Dooney is dead, there's an investigation, and we're prisoners in our own rooms. What a nightmare."

With that, Viv stormed into her room and slammed the door. Okay then. She was clearly upset. I supposed the first order of business tomorrow was to figure out how to get Viv to the village to meet her hat-making idol without Detective Inspector Stewart finding out. Oy.

Chapter 10

"How did you manage to get horses?" Viv asked.

"By not standing around talking about it," I said. I was feeling an intense urgency to get away from the castle and inquiring minds. "Let's go!"

The stables at the castle were for the use of the guests. I had gone down there earlier to charm and disarm the stable master into letting us take out three horses. Viv, Andre and I were suited up in borrowed riding boots, jeans, and thick sweaters—excuse me, jumpers. Why do the Brits call them jumpers?

I had asked Viv the fashion expert when I returned to live in Notting Hill, and she informed me that a "jump" was an old term used for a large men's shirt in the 1800s.

Later, the term was tweaked to "jumper" and is now used to refer to a knitted or crocheted top. Huh.

As we took off for a ride into the village, I glanced at the distant hills dotted with woolly sheep. I saw one jump over a stone wall and thought from that point of origin the term fit. Then I pondered why Americans call knitted tops "sweaters." I had no idea. I realized I was becoming more British every day and knew my English-born mother would be proud.

Now, the constables had been very clear that we weren't to leave the premises but I'd done a little reconnaissance on my phone the day before, and by "recon" I mean I called the local library in the village and asked them if Dominick Falco's address was public information. They assured me it was and gave it to me. Librarians for the win!

With their help, I discovered that Dominick Falco, the hatmaker, lived on the edge of the village closest to the castle. It would be a tragedy for Viv to be so close to him and not be able to visit. All I had to do was find a way off the grounds that would lead to the village. I was hoping there was a break in a hedgerow or something.

Andre and I had discussed my plan over breakfast, and he agreed to lead us since he had the most experience on horseback. I told him no jumps and, even though he looked disappointed, he agreed.

The late-morning air was brisk, and as we trotted past the front of the castle, one of the constables waved us down.

"Names?" he inquired.

"Scarlett Parker, Vivian Tremont and Andre Eisel," I said. "We're just taking a short ride around the castle to clear our heads."

He stared at us, clearly undecided. He was short and stocky with a kindly face, and looked like he was coasting into his golden years. It would be a shame to cause him undue stress.

"Detective Inspector Stewart said it was fine," I said.

"Oh, well then, enjoy your ride," he said. He gave us a cheerful wave and we continued on, branching off onto a narrow lane.

"When did you ask Stewart?" Viv said.

"I'll ask him when we get back," I said. "I'm sure he'll say it's all right."

"We're going to end up in jail," Andre said.

"No, we're not," I said. "We're of no interest to the police."

"Except that you're the one who found the body," Viv said.

"I didn't even know the man," I said. "I'm just a tiny detail in this investigation."

My horse, Mabel, a big brown gal with a black mane and tail, paused to eat some grass. The others trotted on without us. I pulled on the reins and nudged her with my heels.

"Come on, Mabel," I hissed. "You're making me look bad."

She didn't care. She wouldn't budge.

"If you're going to let her eat the entire ride, we'll never get there," Andre called over his shoulder.

"It's not really about 'letting,'" I argued.

Andre trotted back to me. He looked fantastic with his straight posture, his blazer over his sweater and his riding gloves. His big gray mare sidled up next to Mabel, and Andre gave the hungry horse a firm slap on the haunch. Mabel stomped her back feet in protest but took the hint and began to trot down the lane after Viv and her pretty dappled mount. Unprepared, I was left to clutch the reins while my posterior took a beating from the saddle and my hat bounced around my head, sliding over my eyes.

Mabel fell into step with Viv's horse while I shoved my riding hat back on my head. We continued on with Andre cantering up beside us. Mabel was more cooperative now, and I suspected it was because my load was lighter as I'd left my dignity back in that clump of grass. I shifted in my seat, knowing I was going to be sore later.

We followed the property line of the castle. The landscape was breathtaking with rolling hills unfurling with the vibrant green of late spring. I took a deep breath, inhaling the sweetness of the air. This, this was why I'd wanted to come to the country for the weekend.

The castle was a tiny blip on the horizon, and I felt the tension in my shoulders drop as we put more distance between ourselves and the keep. I didn't want to think about Piper May and Dooney Portis and their wedding, which should have been tomorrow. When I'd called Harrison last night to tell him what had happened, he was halfway to his car when I told him not to bother, that we weren't able to leave.

He wasn't thrilled with having me stuck in another

murder investigation and neither was I, but at least I had ruled out the castle as a wedding venue. Even without the murder, it was simply too much, even for me.

"Here," Andre said. He stopped his horse and we came to a halt beside him.

Mabel was being a model of good behavior now, and I was certain it was because she wanted Andre's good opinion of her restored.

"Here what?" Viv asked.

"There's a wooden gate that I think will lead us to the village," he said. He pointed and, sure enough, there was a wide wooden gate offering us an opening in the stone wall that ran the perimeter of the castle property.

"Do you think this is a secret entrance to the castle grounds?" I asked.

"Most likely it's just the path the local farmers use to reach the fields," Andre said. "A shortcut, if you will."

"After you," Viv said.

We left the main path and took the side trail Andre indicated. When we arrived at the gate, we saw it had a simple latch, no lock. We made our way through it, and were free from the castle and headed to the village. Much to Mabel's dismay, we had to ford a small stream, and when we stepped up onto the opposite bank, she stomped her feet, letting me know quite plainly that she was unhappy.

"Do we know where Dominick Falco lives?" Viv asked. "How impolite is it of me to just arrive on his doorstep? After all, he did retire."

"Once a milliner, always a milliner," I said. I took out

my phone and checked his address. He lived at 4 Adelaide Court. The village was small, maybe three thousand people; how hard could he be to find?

I opened an app on my phone and entered the address. The directions led us through town, which was quiet for a Friday morning, and down a side street and then another until we found Adelaide Court. We passed people, but no one paid any mind to the three of us riding on horseback through the middle of the village. You have to love the country.

"I don't see number four," Andre said. "Oh, wait, the numbers are going down."

We followed him along the cobbled road, which was so quaint. The upper stories of the houses lining the street were covered in ivy or sporting hanging flower baskets. The architecture was old, angular redbrick buildings, some of which were painted white, thick wooden shingles for roofs, and multipaned windows that looked out onto the street. I felt as if we'd passed through some portal and stepped back in time.

"There it is," Viv cried. She pointed at a charming cottage up ahead. She stopped her horse and looked at me and said, "I can't do this. Let's go back."

"What?" I cried. "We came all this way and my backside is killing me. We are absolutely doing this."

"But to call without notice," she protested. "It's so rude."

"We're just going to say hello," I said. "If he's busy we can arrange to come back another time. We're stuck here for a few more days anyway."

"All right," Viv said. Her horse rocked back and forth as if sensing her agitation. "But I'm only giving in because I know you'll just badger me to death if I don't."

"That's the spirit," I said.

She dismounted in perfect fluid form, then brushed the dust off her clothes and took off her helmet, fluffing her hair with one hand while tucking the helmet under her elbow with the other.

She handed Andre her reins, as he had offered to watch the horses while we visited Mr. Falco, and then she glanced up at me. "Well, come on then."

"You go ahead," I said. "I'll catch up."

"Catch up?" she asked. "Scarlett, the door is right there."

I glanced at the house. She was right. There was no sidewalk. The front door had a one-step stoop and there it was. We were all of a yard away from the entrance.

"You can't get off the horse, can you?" Andre asked. His mouth puckered to one side as if he was trying hard not to laugh.

"Yes, I can," I said. "I just might need someone to catch me."

"Here," he said. He swung off his horse even more gracefully than Viv. He landed on the ground and looped both his reins and Viv's on the trellis that ran up one side of the house. He came to stand beside Mabel and held out his arms.

"I can't unlock my legs from around the horse," I said.

"Just fall," he said. "I'll catch you."

If this were a trust exercise, I would have no problem

trusting Andre. The problem was a trust exercise was usually done indoors over a squashy carpet. I glanced down at the cobblestones. Despite centuries of use, they still looked as hard as, well, rock.

"I'll catch you, Scarlett," he said. "I promise."

"Fine." I let go of the reins and slid into his arms in a tangle of limbs. It was probably the most awkward dismount in the history of horsemanship.

He set me on my feet and I almost whimpered as pain shot up my thighs.

"Chin up, love," he said. "We still have to ride back."

I glanced around the picturesque village. Surely, there had to be a rideshare service somewhere in this town. I hobbled closer to Viv. She was shaking her head at me when the door opened and a short, round, older man with a thick tuft of white hair stepped out onto the stoop.

"Vivian Tremont," he said. "As I live and breathe. What an extraordinary thing to find you in front of my house."

Vivian's eyes went wide. She opened her mouth to speak but nothing came out. She stood there gaping, which led me to deduce that this was the one and only Dominick Falco.

"Good morning, Mr. Falco," I said. "I'm Scarlett Parker. My cousin Vivian and I and our friend Andre Eisel just happen to be staying at the castle for the weekend, and we took the chance that you might be in residence and willing to take tea with us?"

"Why, I'd be delighted," he said. He reached forward and shook each of our hands, pumping our arms with great enthusiasm. I liked Dominick Falco. He glanced at Andre and said, "Use the alley to bring the horses round back. I have a small yard where you can tend them and they'll be safe and contained while we chat."

"Oh, we don't want to impose," Viv said. The thought of poor manners was enough to break her catatonic state. "We'd be happy to take you to tea in one of the shops." She gestured vaguely at the village.

"And share the famous milliner Vivian Tremont with the common folk?" Mr. Falco asked. There was a twinkle in his eye. "Not a chance. We'll have tea here, much more cozy."

Vivian graced him with a small smile and said, "That's incredibly kind of you."

"Not at all, my housekeeper is the kind one, since she's making the tea," he said. He opened a gate on the side of the house and Andre led the three horses to the back. Then Dominick gestured for Viv and me to follow him inside.

I don't know what I expected a retired milliner's house to look like but it wasn't this. Despite the old-world feel from the outside of the house, the interior was bright and airy, with square-edged furniture, all steel and glass and shaped wood. There was hardly any clutter at all. It was almost midcentury-modern American in its austerity.

Mr. Falco led us through the narrow house to a room at the back. Now, this space made more sense. It was clearly his work area. Despite his being retired, there were several hats in varying stages of completion perched on mannequin heads on a long wooden worktable. The large window looked out over the garden, where we could see Andre tending the horses. A row of birdfeeders hung in front of the window and judging by the way they were swinging, the birds had just taken off, probably at the startling arrival of the horses.

Mr. Falco gestured for us to take a seat at what looked like a conference table. There were scraps of fabric, buttons and bits of lace and other notions littered across the surface. It made me feel at home, like we were in Mim's Whims.

A petite woman entered the room. She looked to be a few years younger than Mr. Falco, with her brown hair threaded with silver.

"Emily, there you are," Mr. Falco said. "Would you be so kind as to fetch a tray of tea and biscuits for our guests?"

"Certainly, Mr. Falco," she said. She glanced at the two of us. "Any dietary restrictions?"

"None for any of us, thank you," Viv said.

I smiled at her and Emily smiled back. She had a saucy dimple in her right cheek that gave her expression just the right amount of impudence.

"Mr. Falco, I can't thank you enough for taking the time to meet with us," Viv said. She clutched her hands to her chest. "I have been an admirer of yours my entire life."

"Please call me Dominick," he said. "And let's pretend you're only sixteen so I don't feel so old."

"Oh, I didn't mean—" Viv stammered. She was rarely flustered so this was a treat for me. I loved Viv dearly but sometimes her placidity could be annoying, especially when I tended to skew dramatic.

Andre knocked on the back door, and I hurried over to open it for him. He wiped his feet on the mat outside and stepped into the room.

"Here, join us, young man." Dominick waved him over to us.

Andre slid into a seat and said, "I'm afraid our horses have made themselves at home in your yard."

We all glanced out the window and saw a big pile of horse droppings. Viv looked mortified but Dominick laughed. "No problem, we'll shovel it right into the flower beds."

He was smiling and I sensed there was very little that upset Dominick Falco. I wondered if that was the beauty of retirement. Speaking of which.

"Forgive me if I'm talking out of turn, Dominick," I said. "But I was under the impression that you'd given up hat making."

Viv shot me a warning look, but that seemed ridiculous since we were sitting in what was clearly a studio and there were hats right over there.

He shrugged. "I still do special-occasion custom designs."

"For very important clientele, I'm guessing," Andre said.

"Queen Silvia of Sweden needed a hat for an event here in London," he said. "She was a longtime supporter of my work, so when she reached out, how could I refuse?"

I glanced back at the table and saw a bright blue hat

with a vibrant yellow trim. I knew those were the colors of the Swedish flag, so I assumed that was hers.

Dominick turned to Viv. "Once the craft is in your blood, you can never really retire."

She nodded. "Our grandmother never retired. She worked in the shop right up until she passed."

"I was a great admirer of her work," Dominick said. "Just as I am of yours."

"You've seen my work?" Viv asked. She looked like she might swoon.

I glanced at Andre. I just knew this was about to become a deep discussion on all things hats, like the body of the hat (hood, capeline or flare) or the type of material used (sisal versus sinamay)—in other words, the conversation was about to get really, really boring. And it did.

Thankfully, Emily showed up several minutes later with the tea tray and, bless her, it was fully loaded with all sorts of scrumptious goodies. I didn't want to make a pig of myself but our ride in the fresh air had me feeling ravenous.

"Come, let me show you my latest," Dominick said to Viv. He seemed giddy to have someone there to talk shop with. He glanced at me and Andre. "Help yourselves. We'll be right back."

They wandered over to the worktable and I grinned at Andre. "You don't have to tell me twice."

He poured the tea while I loaded two plates with warm scones, clotted cream, and fresh apple slices. Heaven.

We ate in companionable silence and I suspected the fresh air had given Andre as big an appetite as mine.

"Do you think she'll be less cranky now?" he asked.

"Yes, right up until we return to the castle," I said. "I can't blame her. A person she knows is dead, potentially murdered, there's no wedding, so our purpose for being here is nonexistent, and the two families tied to the wedding are pretty awful. Plus, being questioned by the police is never fun, as we all know."

"What about the McKenna bride and her curse?" Andre asked.

"You don't really believe in that, do you?" I asked.

"There was a cold spot in the middle of my room last night and there was no reason for it, as both the windows and the door were shut," he said. "I think she's real."

"If she is, she's over one thousand years old. Don't you think she'd have gotten over whatever it is that's bothering her by now? Andre, you don't have to fret. I think it's just an old folktale," I said. I had no idea if it was or wasn't but I didn't want Andre brooding about it for the next few days. "I mean, if it was a true curse, there would have been a lot more incidents at the castle by now."

Viv and Dominick returned to the table, and I was relieved to see that Andre and I had left plenty of food for them. Viv poured a cup of tea and handed it to Dominick, who settled into his seat.

"Are you talking about ghosts?" he asked.

Viv gave us a stern look. "You weren't, were you?"

"Just kicking it around," I said. "I'm trying to convince Andre that the curse of the McKenna bride is just an old ghost story and nothing to worry about."

"Except that there is one very angry ghost who curses

anyone who marries in the castle," Andre said. "And as Archie the caretaker says, she's claimed another."

"That's not exactly how the curse goes," Dominick said.

We all turned to face him, and I asked, "You've heard of it?"

"Of course," he said. "The village is still an extension of the castle, seeing as most of the castle staff live in the village. There was quite the to-do yesterday when the police said no one could leave the castle while they investigated the death of the groom."

He gave us a pointed look and when I glanced at Viv and Andre, I noted they had matching sheepish expressions. I suspected my face looked just like theirs.

"In our defense, we only skived off so we could meet you," I said. I felt like one of the cool kids, using the British slang for "skipping out."

Dominick sipped his tea. He looked amused. "Oh, don't worry, I won't tell a soul that you were here and neither will Emily."

"Thank you," Viv said. "Things are a bit tense at Waverly Castle right now and we appreciate the respite."

A bit tense. You just have to love the British gift of understatement. Still, I was curious about what Dominick knew about the McKenna curse. Archie said she was an unhappy bride who died tragically before her wedding and haunted the castle to this day, but he didn't say much more than that.

"Do you know why the McKenna bride curses any weddings that are meant to be held in the castle?" I asked. "The caretaker said something about her being unhappy, but didn't say why."

146

"I do. It's a sad story," Dominick said. "Brigit Mc-Kenna was a young girl when she was to be married off. Her curse—if it was the curse that killed the groom in this wedding—was that whoever should be forced into a marriage they didn't want would find their way out through death. If the groom did suffer from the curse, it's because he didn't want this wedding."

"Their way out through death?" I repeated. "Are you sure about the curse? Not to be blunt, but he was marrying a fortune, and I don't think he was trying to escape that."

"I agree," Viv said. "Dooney definitely wanted to marry Piper. In fact, he needed to marry her if his family was to survive. I don't think he was sentimental about the reasons. He was fiscally committed to the outcome."

"The curse is very specific," Dominick said. "Let me explain."

We all leaned in, even Andre, and gave him our full attention.

Chapter 11

"Before the Treaty of Union in 1707, the Scots were their own nation and Baron Douglas Mulvaney, the resident of Waverly Castle at the time, decided it was advantageous for himself, a titled landowner, to align himself with one of the more powerful lairds in Scotland through marriage. He offered to marry Laird McKenna's daughter, giving the laird access to the southern portion of England in exchange for a hefty dowry and a young woman who would bear his children."

"Seems normal for the times," Andre said.

"It was," Dominick said. "Women were a sort of currency back in the day."

Viv and I emitted low growls in our throats and Dominick smiled. "I agree completely. Also, according to the records, Baron Mulvaney was fifty-three years old at the time whilst his would-be bride Brigit McKenna was at the tender age of fourteen. You can imagine her dismay that he was not exactly a handsome young swain."

"He was thirty-nine years older? The horror. So, what happened?" I asked. I was impatient to hear the details, not that I believed in the curse, but I was extremely curious.

"Brigit refused to marry the baron," Dominick said.

"I'm guessing that was frowned upon," Viv said. She nibbled at a scone with cream.

"It was," Dominick said. "Along with other unsavory punishments, they locked her in the castle tower until she complied."

"It's always the tower," Andre said. "I'm guessing she didn't comply."

"No," Dominick said. "Instead, she cursed the baron to remain childless his entire life."

"Fitting," I said. I liked Brigit's spunk.

"She also cursed any matrimony that should take place in the castle, stating if a person was forced to marry against their will, may they escape such a fate in death."

"Well," Andre said. That was all he said, as if he'd run out of words. I was right there with him. Could Dooney have died because—

No. I shook my head. I didn't believe in curses. Ghosts, maybe. But not curses, not ones left behind and not from the other side of the veil.

"Which is why my assumption was that if it was the curse that caused the groom—Dooney, did you say?—to pass, then he was the one who didn't want to marry," Dominick said.

He calmly helped himself to a finger sandwich as if he hadn't just told us there was a vengeful ghost haunting the castle that we were presently staying in.

The conversation returned to millinery, and Andre and I listened while Dominick and Viv became best friends for life over their shared passion. I started to get antsy when we'd been gone more than an hour. I did not want our absence noticed.

When there was a break in the discussion of embellishments, I said, "It has been such a pleasure to meet you, Dominick." I was using my *let's wrap it up* voice and Viv frowned at me. I ignored her.

"I'll go ready the horses," Andre said. He rose from his seat and held out his hand to Dominick. "Thank you for your hospitality. It's been a treat."

"My pleasure," Dominick said. "Do come again."

Sensing that he and Viv wanted to chat just a little bit longer, I said, "I'll help you, Andre." Then I turned to Dominick and echoed Andre's sentiments, shook his hand and said, "If you're ever in London, please come visit us in Notting Hill."

He smiled and his eyes twinkled. "I might just do that."

Andre led me out to the backyard, which smelled fragrantly horsey.

"What do you make of that?" Andre asked.

I stood stroking Mabel's nose and neck, hoping to win her over before we rode home, while Andre readied the saddles and bridles.

"Dominick the person? Or what Dominick had to say about the McKenna bride and her curse?"

"The curse, obviously the curse," he said. He sounded overwrought.

"Well, I don't believe in the curse," I said. I don't think I was imagining the way that Andre's shoulders dropped in relief. "But he might not have been wrong about Dooney wanting out of the marriage."

Andre's eyebrows lifted. "Go on."

"I just can't help noticing the similarities," I said. "Piper was marrying into an old family, a branch of the nobility, and in return, Dooney was saving the Portis family reputation with a huge infusion of cash."

"Much like Brigit was to marry the baron to give her father an ally in the south and sons for the baron's legacy," Andre said.

"In a sense, both Brigit McKenna and Dooney Portis were pawns. It's weird, right?" I asked.

"Definitely, uncomfortably similar," he said. He scooped up the reins of the two horses and handed me Mabel's. "Come on, time to go back before Detective Inspector Stewart notices we're gone."

Viv met us in front of the house and, with a fond wave to Dominick, who stood in his open doorway, we headed out.

As much as I was enjoying the outing with Viv and Andre, I was dreading how sore I would be after the ride back. Thankfully, the sound of the horses' hooves on the cobblestones and the dreamy spring day in the English countryside took my mind off my aches. I pondered the castle as we slipped back onto the path around the meadow and headed toward it.

The main part sat impressively on top of the motte. It had one central tower in the same heavy beige stone as the rest of the building. My eyes scanned the top. Was that where Brigit had jumped from? Was it the very same tower, or had it been rebuilt over the years?

"That'd be one heck of a fall," Andre said.

I glanced over at him and saw he was staring up at the tower as well. Below the crenellated top, windows were carved into the stone. Had one of those rooms belonged to Brigit? Is that where she was kept until she complied? My eyes dropped to the ground where she would have fallen. No wonder she haunted the castle. I would, too.

"Poor thing," Viv said. "What a horrible choice to have to make—death, or being the chattel of some perverted old man who wanted her solely for the purpose of bearing sons."

"Agreed." I couldn't help but feel terrible for Brigit, just a child herself, having to make such a choice.

It occurred to me that I had forgotten to ask Dominick one very important question. Both he and Archie had talked about the curse of the McKenna bride but neither one had mentioned any other bride or groom who'd died before their wedding at Waverly Castle.

"Do you think Dooney is the first?" I asked.

"First what?" Viv asked.

"First groom to die?" I asked. "For that matter, was he the first person in a wedding to die from the curse, apart from Brigit? Because both Archie and Dominick talked

153

about the McKenna bride and her curse, but they didn't mention any other bride or groom dying in the castle. Doesn't that seem strange? I mean, wouldn't you say that there's this curse and you know it's true because Donna in 1745, Phyllis in 1862 and Sharon in 1934 all died when they were about to get married at Waverly Castle?"

"Donna, Phyllis, Sharon?" Andre asked with a laugh. "Where did you get those names?"

"They were the first ones to pop into my head," I said.

"Phyllis sounds like someone's pony," Viv said.

"And Donna is their goose," Andre laughed.

"Then what's Sharon?" Viv asked.

"Their goat," Andre said.

"Those were just examples," I said. I felt the need to defend myself and keep us on point. "You have to admit, it's a valid question."

"Fine," Viv said. "All dubious name choices aside, yes, it is strange that neither of them mentioned anyone else dying right before their wedding. For the legend of the curse to have lasted over a thousand years, there should be a reason for it."

"Can we ask Archie?" Andre asked. "He seems fairly invested in the castle."

"I think we should," I said. "I believe he's warming up to me. Finding a body together will do that to people."

"It's a grave mistake," Andre said. I glanced at him in dismay, thinking he couldn't be serious and . . . he wasn't.

"Oh, ha ha, very punny," I said.

"Andre is right," Viv said. "Friendship has to be urned."

Andre burst out laughing. "Good one."

"Stop it, both of you," I chastised them. I waited a beat and added, "This is dead serious."

They both looked at me. Not even a twitch of the lips.

"Aw, come on, you know that was solid wordplay," I said.

"It's all right, Scarlett," Andre said kindly. "You get points for trying."

I glowered. We were riding past the castle now and headed for the stables. No one had chased us down, or yelled at us, so I was feeling confident that our outing had remained a secret.

When we stopped beside the stables, one of the grooms came out and gathered our reins, holding the horses in place while we dismounted. Andre, without being asked, came and stood by my horse. I slid off Mabel, no more gracefully than the last time, and he caught me and set me gently on the ground.

"Thank you," I said to Mabel. I patted the mare's neck in appreciation. "It's been real, girl."

I took a step and tried not to wince but failed miserably. Pain shot down my legs from my hamstrings to my heels. I knew I was going to be limping my way back to the castle. We deposited our borrowed gear in the tack room.

I fell in beside Andre and Viv. Annoyingly, neither of them appeared to be suffering any ill effects from our time on horseback. We rounded the corner of the stone building, when a man stepped out from the shadows, causing all three of us to start. Detective Inspector Stewart.

"Did you have a nice ride?" he asked. He was wearing

a beige overcoat with the same clothes he'd had on last night, his hair was mussed, and he had dark circles under his eyes. I wondered if he'd slept at all.

Viv put her hand on her heart, Andre took a deep breath, and I said, "What's the big idea leaping out at us like that, Detective?"

I wasn't usually cross with people, but my rear end hurt really badly! I rubbed my hands over the back of my thighs. Mercy, my muscles were screaming.

Detective Stewart narrowed his eyes at me and said, "Not much of a rider, are you?"

"What, did my limp give it away?"

"A bit," he said. He pressed his lips together as if trying not to smile. "You might want to stretch it out, do some lunges or a forward bend."

I looked at him doubtfully. "Are you a rider?"

"I am as a matter of fact," he said. He shrugged off his coat and handed it to Viv, who took it without argument. "Try this."

He then struck a pose like a warrior asana in yoga. I did not want to do this to my poor body but he stared at me expectantly.

I sighed and assumed the posture. He coached me to breathe through it and then we switched sides. He then had me do a forward bend. Not going to lie, it hurt like a beast at first but as I breathed, I felt the muscles slowly give and relax.

"Now go take a hot bath," he said when I straightened up. "You'll be right as rain."

I took a few tentative steps. The screaming pain had lessened to a dull aching throb.

"Thank you," I said.

"Don't mention it." He retrieved his coat from Viv and said, "Now why did the three of you go into town to talk to Dominick Falco?"

Viv blinked in surprise. "Did you have us followed?"

"Didn't need to," he said. "One of the constables was in the village and recognized you. He called me and let me know you had left the castle grounds despite my very clear instructions that no one was to leave."

I felt as if the three of us had been called to the principal's office. I was the people person in the group, so I knew it was up to me to explain.

"This is my fault, Detective," I said. Both Viv and Andre started to protest but I held up my hand to stop them. "I'm sure you're aware that Dominick Falco is a hatmaker, a quite famous one in fact."

"I am," he agreed.

"And my cousin is a hatmaker," I said. "So, obviously, when we knew we were coming to Sussex for the wedding, I promised Viv that she could meet Dominick Falco. I'm sorry we left the grounds, and I understand that we shouldn't have, but since we're not suspects . . ."

My voice trailed off. I didn't feel like I needed to hammer home the point that we were just collateral damage and really should be released because obviously none of us had a reason to murder Dooney.

"Who said you're not suspects? Did I say that? Did one

of the constables say that?" Detective Stewart asked. He lifted one eyebrow higher than the other.

"No, but clearly, we're not. We're just two hatmakers and a photographer," I said. I smiled at him. He didn't return it. I felt my smile slip.

"While I appreciate that you, Ms. Parker, do not have any prior connection to Dooney Portis, the same can't be said of your friends," he said. "And given the way this case has gone, that makes them suspects."

Detective Stewart turned and began to stride to the castle, clearly expecting us to keep up. I exchanged a glance with Viv and Andre and the three of us picked up our pace.

"Excuse me, but suspects? You actually just called them suspects," I said. I saw both Viv and Andre shake their heads, but I ignored them. "What are you implying?"

"I'm not implying anything," Detective Stewart said. "The medical examiner has made a preliminary determination that Dooney Portis was murdered, and their relationships with the deceased make them suspects."

Viv blinked in surprise at his blunt speech. The detective glanced at her and then Andre, who also looked taken aback by the detective's tactlessness. I knew he was thinking about the ghost and the curse, and I really hoped he didn't say anything and make us sound like a bunch of ghost-hunting weirdos.

"How was he murdered?" I asked. I'd seen Dooney. The memory of finding him was burned in my brain. There were no bruises, no marks, no pool of blood, nothing. There had been nothing to indicate that he hadn't just died of a brain aneurysm or something.

"I'm not at liberty to discuss the details," Detective Stewart said. "But it has come to my attention that both Ms. Tremont and Mr. Eisel have a history with Mr. Portis."

"History?" Andre cried. His voice was much higher than normal. "No, there's no history with me and Dooney."

"Didn't you go to the same primary school?" Detective Stewart asked. He studied Andre closely.

"Well, yes, but—"

"And didn't he bully you?"

Andre stopped walking and his jaw dropped. "How do you know this? Dooney didn't even recognize me when I took his engagement photos."

"Oh, yes, he did," Detective Stewart said. "He told his bride-to-be that he had bullied you in school. In fact, it was why he insisted that you be their photographer. According to his fiancée, he was trying to make amends and he thought that being the photographer for the wedding of the year would be a way to do it."

Andre looked as if the detective had just sucker punched him. I reached out and squeezed his arm in support.

"So, tell me, Mr. Eisel, were you here to exact revenge for the childhood torment he inflicted upon you?" He stepped forward and loomed over Andre, looking impressive with his overcoat billowing about him. "Did you murder Dooney Portis?"

"What? No! That's mental," Andre cried. "I would never."

"He would never," I seconded.

The detective stepped back. "Where were you during the cocktail party?"

"He was with us," Viv said. "He escorted us from our rooms to the cocktail party and he was with us the entire time."

The detective turned to her. His tone was gentler with Viv, naturally, as she had that uncanny ability to soften everyone—men, women, detectives.

"And what about you, Ms. Tremont?" he asked.

"What about me?" Viv met his gaze, looking bored.

"Is it true that you and Mr. Portis had a relationship?"

"When you say 'relationship,' what exactly do you mean?" she asked. She gave him side-eye as if he'd just sprouted mushrooms out of his ears.

"Were you involved . . ." Detective Stewart paused as if looking for the correct word. "Intimately?"

Viv stared at him. It was a withering look, chillier than an arctic wind. I felt myself shrink and noticed Andre hunkered into his blazer, too. To his credit, Detective Stewart did not flinch. Instead, he met her stare and waited without blinking. I would have bet ten British pounds that it took every ounce of stamina he had to pull that off.

"No." Viv drew out the lone syllable, making her disdain for the question clear. If Detective Stewart was smart, he'd understand immediately that she would not entertain this question again. "I know . . . knew . . . him only through Piper, who is a longtime acquaintance."

"Forgive me," Detective Stewart said. "There were rumors."

"Rumors?" she asked. "Anyone who suggested that anything intimate happened between me and Dooney

Portis is either trying to stir the pot, or is woefully mis-informed."

"I see," Detective Stewart said. He rocked back on his heels as if considering her words. It didn't matter one lit-tle bit to Viv what he thought.

"Good day, Detective," she said. She began to walk to the castle and gestured for Andre and me to follow.

Andre and I fell in behind her. Honestly, I felt as if I were a lady-in-waiting to the queen, heading back to her palace. It was kind of cool. I glanced over my shoulder once and saw Detective Stewart watching us. I did not like the speculative look in his eye.

Chapter 12

"Ginger, I'm coming to get you," Harry said. "It's absolutely ridiculous that you have to stay in the castle when there's been a murder."

"They still won't let us leave," I said. I was grateful to hear Harry's voice even if it was just over the phone. "And I'm not sure how they determined that he was murdered. Honestly, I didn't see anything that indicated Dooney had been killed. He looked passed out drunk or asleep. It's all very bewildering, and I think we're stuck here until Sunday."

I was sitting on a bench in the garden by a lily pond while Andre wandered about taking pictures of whatever struck his fancy and Viv sketched ideas for future hats. I had never felt my lack of a creative outlet so keenly. I wondered if I should take up knitting or crochet.

"But that's rubbish," Harry protested. "You have nothing to do with Dooney's murder."

"I know that, and you know that, but the detective is being very thorough," I said. "No one is allowed to leave."

"And yet you still managed to go and meet Dominick Falco," he said. He sounded amused. He'd never admit it, but I think Harry enjoyed my shenanigans.

"Well, it was for Viv's mental health," I said. "So I figured it was worth the risk of getting into trouble."

"Did you?" he asked. "Get into trouble?"

"Detective Stewart wasn't thrilled that we'd left the grounds but he didn't haul us in for questioning or arrest us if that's what you mean."

"I can't believe the risk he's taking by keeping you all there. I mean, there's a killer in that castle and if anyone else gets murdered—" His voice trailed off. I could hear the frustration pouring off him even over the phone. "I'm going to call Alistair and see what we can do."

"Thank you," I said. "It's nice to have someone on the outside. Now how's Bella?"

"Bella from hella misses you," he said. "Also, she chewed up my new trainers."

"The pair?" I asked.

"Just the left one," he said.

"Do you think it tasted better than the right one?" I joked.

"Perhaps it had more sole," he returned.

"Heel-arious." I groaned. He laughed, and I felt as if I'd achieved a victory. This was why I had to marry Harry. He was the only one who laughed at my puns, and it had taken me years to get him to this point. I clearly could never leave him. "Send me pictures of her. I miss her."

"Ahem." He cleared his throat.

"And you, too, of course," I said.

"Thank you," he said. "I miss you, too. I still think I should come down."

"I don't think they'll let you in. Besides, I doubt they'll keep us here past Sunday," I said. "I assume since we were all staying here anyway and it's a murder investigation, that they'll keep us until Sunday, but I can't imagine they'll demand that several dozen people stay in a castle for longer than they originally planned. I mean, who would pay for it?"

"That could be why Detective Stewart is pushing so hard," Harry said. "He's on a time crunch."

"So, I'll see you on Sunday, unless we're let out early for good behavior," I said.

"I'll be there on Sunday," he said. "If not sooner."

We exchanged "I love yous" and I ended the call. I missed Harry. I missed our apartment—excuse me, our flat—in Notting Hill. While Sussex was lovely, minus the murder, and I enjoyed breathing in the country air, I missed our life. I missed Fee and the hat shop and the Saturday market. In short, I wanted to go home.

"How's Harrison?" Viv asked.

"Concerned," I said. "He wants to come and get us now."

"I hope you told him yes," she said.

"Why? They're not going to let us go and he'd just be stuck here, too," I said. "Besides, who would look after Bella?"

"Fee could watch her," Viv said.

"On top of watching the hat shop?" I asked. "That feels like taking advantage."

"She loves Bella," Viv said.

"That doesn't mean she wants to dog sit," I said.

Viv waved me off, and I stood, stretched and followed the gravel path to where Andre was tossing pebbles into the lily pond. I was still sore from our morning ride but at least I wasn't limping. I glanced at Andre. He looked contemplative and I wondered if I should interrupt his thoughts. Then I went ahead and did it, because what are friends for?

"Why are you glaring at the pond? Has it done something to offend you?" I asked.

His head jerked up as if I'd startled him. "No, although it needs a good dredging."

I glanced at the pond. He was right. It was thick with algae, too thick, and it emitted an off-putting smell.

"If it's not the pond . . ." I let my words trail off, waiting for him to share.

"He knew who I was," Andre said. "That toe-rag recognized me."

"Dooney?" I asked just to clarify. I had wondered if he'd been upset when the detective mentioned that Dooney remembered bullying him in school and had told his fiancée.

"Yes, and what a load of codswallop that he was trying to make amends for tormenting me as a kid," he said. His nostrils flared. "I went through that entire engagement photo shoot feeling sick to my stomach and he could have made it all go away by simply apologizing."

"Maybe he didn't know how to," I suggested. "Or maybe he thought you didn't remember him."

"As if I could forget the bloke who mocked the way I walked and talked, who stuffed me into a bin and stole my best jumper."

"I'm sorry he was cruel to you," I said.

"Thank you," Andre said. He glanced from the pool up to the castle. "I don't believe he changed. It was much more in character to have him go ahead with the photo shoot, knowing that it would upset me, and pretend not to know me so he could enjoy my excruciating discomfort and not be called to account. I should have refused to take the pictures. I should have yelled at him or punched him in the mouth."

I put my hand on his arm, trying to soothe his temper. He had every right to be angry. I thought about the smarmy Dooney who had knocked on our door to talk to Viv. He'd clearly wanted her to feel jealous that he was marrying Piper, which was ridiculous. It had been so obvious that what he accused Viv of—pining for him—was what *he'd* been doing, pining for *her.* Dooney was not someone who felt empathy, and the idea that he'd wanted Andre to be his photographer to make amends was laughable. I knew in my heart Andre was right. Dooney wanted him there to torture him.

"Yeah, I don't think he changed either," I said.

"I appreciate your support," Andre said. He put his

arm around my shoulders, pulled me into a half hug and kissed the top of my head. I hugged him back.

"It's not just that I support you, although I do one hundred percent," I said. "The fact is, he was murdered. That seems a solid indicator that he never changed his bullying ways and someone had finally had enough."

"Agreed."

"The question that remains is, Who else is here that he bullied to the point where they felt compelled to murder him to be rid of him?"

We stared at each other for a moment and then glanced up at the castle. The centuries-old pile of rocks was keeping secrets, and if we wanted to get out of here, we needed to try to figure out exactly what they were.

"Why do we have to eat in the dining room?" Viv asked. We closed the door to our suite and walked down the passageway to the stairs.

"I suspect because the detective wants it that way," Andre said. "What better opportunity will he have to observe everyone all together?"

We'd been informed by one of the castle staff that tonight's dinner was being served as if it were the rehearsal dinner because they already had the menu planned and the food shouldn't go to waste. The dining room had been set up for the rehearsal dinner well in advance, so it was also easier on the staff to stick to the original plan. It was sound reasoning, but I suspected that Andre's theory was more accurate.

"But we're just hatmakers and a photographer," I said. "And I'm not even really a hatmaker. I'm just here to . . ."

"Smooth things out when I'm rude to people," Viv said.

"Yeah, that," I agreed. Viv smiled at me, and I felt our unbreakable cousin bond thrum between us.

"I suppose we need to look on the bright side," Andre said.

"A man was murdered, you two are potential suspects, and you think there's a bright side?" I asked.

"Yes."

"Which would be what?" Viv asked.

"There'll be free booze with dinner," he said.

He wasn't wrong.

Two bottles of wine, a red and a white, were placed on every table, and the waitstaff started buzzing around the room. I had heard the castle staff were given an entire wing to stay in and I wondered how they felt about it. The kitchen staff clearly brought their A game, as dinner was delicious. It started with a crab and langoustine fresh herb salad, followed by lamb, spring vegetables and roasted potatoes. After the day of horseback riding, murder accusations and fresh air in the garden, I was ravenous.

Again, we shared our table with the May cousins, who didn't greet us and spoke only among themselves. Even my most extroverted self could not charm them into conversation. I went so far as to comment on the weather, as every Brit can dish about the weather for at least a minute. Not these folks.

The atmosphere in the dining room could only be described as oppressive. I had the sense that everyone was shoveling their food in as fast as they could so that they could escape back to their rooms.

Much to my surprise, both the May and Portis families, including Piper, were in attendance. To me, this was taking the "keep calm and carry on" sentiment a bit too far. If it were me, and my groom was found dead and foul play was suspected, I'd be ripping the castle apart brick by brick, trying to find his killer.

Both families had new faces at their tables. Men in suits, who looked somber and serious and very protective. Had to be their attorneys. I supposed if the families weren't allowed to leave the castle while the investigation was happening, then it only made sense that they brought their lawyers in to protect their interests. Still, it was unsettling.

I took a bite of my perfectly roasted potatoes and glanced at Piper. I didn't want to stare but she looked distraught. Her complexion was gray, she had dark circles under her eyes, her hair was in a messy bun, and she was wearing a navy blue chemise that I suspected was her mother's, as it seemed a bit loose and, frankly, matronly.

She moved her food around with her fork, and never lifted her gaze from her plate. The misery pouring off her made my heart pinch. I didn't know if she had loved Dooney but she certainly looked stricken with grief. Whether it was for Dooney or the lost chance to leap up into high society, I couldn't say.

Both Andre and Viv were unusually quiet, and I wondered if the detective telling them that they were suspects was making them feel self-conscious. While I completely understood it and expected nothing less, the somberness that permeated every inch of the room was giving me indigestion.

"Shh." A hiss sounded from the table where the bridesmaids were seated. All eyes turned toward the noise. I scanned the table until I saw Sunny. Her face was flushed even though her glass of wine was untouched. She was staring at Trisha, who had an empty glass of wine in one hand and the bottle in the other.

"Don't you dare shush me," Trisha said.

Sunny's mouth tightened as if she wanted to yell at the other woman but didn't want to make a scene. It looked like she was hanging on to her good manners by a thread.

Trisha suddenly stood up. She shoved her chair back from the table with her backside. The legs of the chair scraped across the floor in a high-pitched squeak. Now everyone was staring at their table.

"How about a toast?" Trisha cried.

"Sit down, Trisha," Quentin, the best man, ordered from the adjacent table, but she didn't listen. Much like Piper, he looked as if he hadn't slept, and his suit was wrinkled, his hair was mussed, and stubble covered his chin.

Trisha ignored him. She began to walk through the tables. She was wobbling on her very pointy heels, and she leaned heavily against the back of a man's chair. He tried to take the wine bottle from her but she laughed and spun away from him.

"A toast to Dooney," she said. She splashed some wine into her glass and raised it high.

It was clear no one knew what to do. I glanced at Dooney's parents and Davina looked pained, but she lifted her glass, which was the signal for everyone else to do the same.

"You will be missed," Trisha said.

"To Dooney," the crowd murmured.

Not knowing what else to do, Viv, Andre and I joined the toast. Everyone drank and I hoped that this was the end of it. It wasn't.

"Wait," Trisha cried. She spun around so that she was facing the bridesmaid table. "I have one more thing to say."

I glanced from her to the table of women. Sunny was staring at her with a wide-eyed fearful gaze, like a songbird staring down a sparrow hawk. Sunny slowly shook her head, and Trisha laughed.

"Oh, come on, Sunny, we need to toast little Dooney. Don't you think it's only fitting that since we're forced to mourn the man, we should celebrate his child?"

The room went utterly still. Viv and I exchanged a glance. What was Trisha saying? Was she insinuating that Sunny was having Dooney's child? There was vicious and cruel, but this was so over-the-top nasty that it took my breath away.

"Trisha, you're drunk," Piper said. She stood and tossed her napkin down on the table. "Someone take her to her room."

"You don't believe me, Piper?" Trisha taunted her. "Ask her. Ask her why she's gained a stone in the past few months, and why Dooney insisted she be in your wedding party. Ask her what her friendship with Dooney really entailed. I dare you."

"What are you talking about, Trisha?" Piper snapped. She was visibly shaking. She looked at Sunny, who burst into tears.

"Excuse me, I'm not feeling well." Sunny sobbed and ran from the room.

"To baby Dooney," Trisha said. She raised her wineglass high and downed the contents in one swallow. She was the only one to drink.

Dooney's parents rose from their seats and left the room, looking as if they'd just been slapped. Piper's parents tried to get their daughter to follow but she shook them off, approaching Trisha instead.

"How could you do this?"

"You should be thanking me," Trisha said. "You look like a fool, mourning a man who's been having an affair behind your back with his 'special lady friend.' That's what she is, you know. Not the childhood friend he pretended she was, but rather, she's his mistress, she has been for a long time, and now she's having his baby."

Piper drew herself up. "I don't believe you, but even if I did, this was how you thought to tell me? You wanted to humiliate me on the night that should have been one of the happiest of my life?"

"Sorry. It just felt like the right time for the truth," Trisha said. She didn't bother pouring the wine into her glass but drank it straight out of the bottle. Classy. "After all, aren't most murders done by the person the victim is closest to?"

"Are you accusing me of murdering Dooney?" Piper asked. Then she laughed. It was a brittle sound that made my shoulders rise up around my ears. "What about you? You've been in love with Dooney for years but he never gave you the time of day. He never even looked at you. Not once. You've been furious with me ever since we started dating and you've been livid since he proposed.

"That's why I don't believe you for a hot second about Sunny and Dooney. This is just some twisted lie you've cooked up to hurt me. Well, you can't, Trisha. The man I love is dead, and there is nothing you can do that can hurt me more than that. And if I find comfort in anything, it's knowing that you loved him but he never ever loved you. He thought you were pathetic."

"That's not true. He liked me. We were friends," Trisha said. She looked stricken. Piper had clearly struck a nerve.

"Oh, no, you weren't," Piper said. "He used to make fun of you behind your back. Do you want to know what he called you?"

"Shut up, Piper!"

"No, I don't think I will," Piper said. "Since we're spilling the tea, I'm sure you'll be thrilled to know that he said you reminded him of a praying mantis, an unwieldy freak of nature."

"You're lying," Trisha accused. She was furious. Her chest was heaving and I wondered if she was going to take a swing at Piper with the wine bottle. Piper must have had the same thought because she neatly stepped out of range.

"I'm not," Piper said. "Lying is *your* specialty and now everyone knows it. Do you honestly think anyone here

174

believes that Dooney would have had an affair with Sunny?"

"He did!" Trisha snapped.

"No, he didn't," Piper said. With every word, she became the force of nature she was known to be. She stood taller, her chin lifted, and she glared down at Trisha. "You should be ashamed of yourself. If Sunny is pregnant, it's not with Dooney's child, and it's her business and hers alone. You had no right to cause such a scene, using her to humiliate me because you're consumed with jealousy."

"I'm not!" Trisha insisted.

"Please." Piper's gaze ran over her in a look of such scathing contempt, I was surprised Trisha didn't blister with third-degree burns. "If anyone is a suspect in Dooney's murder, it's the woman who's been carrying a torch for him who just can't bear to watch him marry another. Now take your lies and get out of my sight."

Trisha must have seen something truly scary in Piper's expression because she put down the bottle of wine and her glass on the nearest table and headed for the exit, sobbing as she went. Piper's parents rose from their seats and flanked her, and the three of them left the dining room as one. As soon as the door shut behind them, it took only half a beat for the room to erupt into chatter.

"I don't think I've ever endured a more uncomfortable social situation in my entire life," Andre said.

"Me either," I said. "And I'm the party crasher."

"What? Did you say you're the party crasher?" one of the May cousins asked.

Uh-oh.

I laughed. It sounded forced. "I'm just teasing him."

I needed to shut this down immediately. I hadn't spent the past few years trying to distance myself from the viral video that had made me infamous only to have it come back to haunt me because of my own big mouth.

"But you're American and a redhead," the woman said. "I thought you looked familiar."

She was in her twenties with mousy brown hair, glasses and a slight overbite.

"There's loads of redheads in America," I said. I picked up my phone and glanced at the display. "Oh, look at the time. Have to dash and get my beauty rest. Viv? Andre?"

As one, the three of us rose from our chairs. I noticed the May cousin was on her phone. Probably looking for the video. Ack!

"Good night," I said. Viv and Andre repeated the sentiment and we headed for the door.

We reached it at the same time as Detective Stewart. He paused to study us.

"Retiring early?" he asked. I couldn't tell if he was just being polite or if he was asking us the question with some sort of intent, as in, were we murderers who were skulking off to hide in our rooms after a big scene?

"It's been a long day," I said. There were no words for how desperately I wanted out of there and the good detective was standing between me and my escape.

"Ms. Parker, Ms. Tremont, Mr. Eisel." Jenkins popped up in the doorway. "There is a gentleman here to see you."

The three of us exchanged a glance. We weren't expecting anyone.

"We discussed this, Mr. Jenkins. No one is allowed in the castle," Detective Stewart said. He sounded annoyed.

"Ginger!"

I knew that voice. I glanced past Jenkins and there was Harry, striding toward me. I'd never been so happy to see anyone in my life.

Chapter 13

"You've infuriated Detective Stewart," I said.

Harry shrugged. There had been a very tense discussion between them. Harry had kept Alistair on the phone during the conversation, with Alistair threatening all sorts of legal repercussions if the detective didn't let Harry stay. Alistair's argument was that we were mere bystanders of Dooney's murder and with a murderer clearly still in the castle, our health and well-being were at risk. Surely, the detective didn't want to jeopardize the safety of one of London's most famous hat designers who was a favorite of the royal family, an up-and-coming photographer and an American whose demise might cause an international incident.

Detective Stewart reluctantly gave in and allowed Harry

to stay. Viv beamed, quite pleased that her new boyfriend, Alistair, had been so effective. Because we now had another person to accommodate, Harry and I took Andre's room while Andre stayed in my room so that neither he nor Viv would be alone. He said it was because there was a murderer in the castle, but I think it was mostly that he was afraid of the ghost of the McKenna bride.

"Fee, Nick, Alistair and I talked about it and none of us could relax, knowing that there was a potential murderer on the premises," he said. "We argued about which one of us should come, but I won."

"Clearly," I said. He looked very proud of himself and I smiled. "How did you manage that?"

"Because I'm the one engaged to you," he said. We were halfway up the main staircase, carrying Harry's things in from his car. I had his laptop satchel while he carried his overnight bag. My man packed light.

"What does that mean exactly?" I blinked at him. "I feel like there's a subtext there that I'm not getting."

"How can I put this delicately?" Harry paused on the landing at the top of the stairs and faced me. "You have an extraordinary knack for getting into trouble."

My jaw dropped. "I think I've been slandered."

"Perhaps 'knack' is the wrong word and I should say 'gift.' You have a gift for entering dangerous situations," he said. I lifted one eyebrow and he added, "Better?"

"Not really. But I am very glad it's you who came," I said. I kissed him quick and he smiled. "Is Bella staying with Fee?"

"Yes, and they were both delighted," he said.

"Fee is going to spoil her."

"Ridiculously," he agreed. "It's worth it, though. I was useless at the office, fearing you might get murdered in your sleep or something."

"Oh, that's oddly sweet," I said.

He hugged me close, and I had to admit I felt braver with him here. The castle was quiet, unnaturally so. It seemed everyone had turned in early after the big scene at dinner.

I wondered if Sunny was in her room and how she was doing. What Trisha had done to her was about the meanest thing I'd ever witnessed. At the same time, I thought about how Sunny had been hidden between the bookshelves where Dooney was murdered. I only had her word that she'd arrived after I found the body and went to get help with Archie.

What if Trisha was right and Sunny was pregnant with Dooney's child and he rejected Sunny and their baby? Could she have murdered him in revenge? It didn't seem likely given how passive Sunny seemed, but perhaps she'd been pushed too far and felt her only recourse was to murder the man who had rejected her. I shivered.

Harry slid his arm around me and pulled me close, probably thinking my chill was from the cold. The castle never felt truly warm. I tried to tell myself that Dooney's death wasn't my business, but with my friends being considered potential suspects, it was a hard sell to my overactive conscience.

"Do you think we'll be able to leave tomorrow?" I asked. The wedding would have been tomorrow.

"I don't know," Harry said. "Alistair is working his local contacts to see if he can spring us, so we'll have to hope for the best."

I opened the door to the room that was formerly Andre's. It was smaller than the suite I'd shared with Viv, but it was still a beautiful room done in soft shades of sage green. I gestured for Harry to go in first as he had the bigger bag. I followed him and turned to close the door. I glanced down the hallway in both directions to confirm it was clear before shutting the door tight and turning the lock.

Breakfast was held, buffet-style, in a smaller room on the first floor of the castle. Great big warming pans of eggs and sausage, scones and toast, and urns of tea and coffee were a welcome start to the day.

Harry and I loaded our plates and joined Viv and Andre, who were already seated beside a window that looked out over the castle gardens. The sun was streaming through the pane, making even the somber day bright. The gardens looked thick and lush with greenery and blooms that were just beginning to burst. It was a perfect day for a wedding. I couldn't imagine what Piper was feeling at this moment.

"Morning," Viv greeted us. "How was your night?"

"Quiet," I said. "I conked out as soon as my head hit the pillow. You?"

"Same," she said.

I glanced at Andre and he said, "I expected to hear the

McKenna bride moaning and groaning her way through the halls, but no, so I slept just fine. I did overhear some goss while getting my food this morning, however."

"Oh?" I asked. I took a long sip of my coffee, hoping to get my brain to kick in. I liked tea and all but I needed the punch in the face that was a hot cup of coffee to get my morning started.

"Sunny is missing," he said.

"What?"

He nodded. "I overheard Detective Stewart saying that after she ran out of the dining room last night, she just disappeared. She never went back to her room and a thorough search of the castle hasn't revealed her whereabouts either. Of course, Trisha has proclaimed that this proves that she murdered Dooney and she's now on the run."

I glanced at a small table in the corner where Trisha was sitting alone. She looked rough, and I suspected the hangover she was suffering from was a doozy. I nearly felt sorry for her but I just couldn't manage it. The grief she had caused both families and Sunny was inexcusable.

"I wonder if she's hiding in a place that isn't obvious," Harry said. He turned and looked at me and raised his eyebrows. He was talking about the hidden tunnel.

"Maybe," I said. "Should we try and look for her?"

"Oh, no." Andre shook his head. "Have you never watched a horror film in your life? That's how people die. You never go looking for the missing person."

"This isn't a horror film," I said.

"No, it's worse," he said. "There is an actual murderer in this castle and I, for one, am not rushing to meet them."

"The sooner the case is solved, the sooner we get to leave," Viv said.

Andre raised his hands in the air in exasperation. "Do not come at me with logic."

Viv laughed. She leaned forward and said, "The castle is huge. Why don't we split into two teams and try to cover as much area as we can?"

"Excellent," I said. I pointed to everyone's plates. "Fortify."

"Waverly Castle is four stories," Harry said. "I think we should just divide the floors. Ginger and I will take the odd floors, and you two take the even floors."

We were standing in the lobby of the castle. He handed a visitor's map to Andre, who studied it for a moment and said, "Oh, Viv, we get the music room and the conservatory, oh, and the rose salon."

"Yay!" Viv said. "One question. What do we do if we find Sunny?"

"Call us, and I'll come talk to her," I said. "You have your cell phones?"

They both nodded.

"Let's plan to meet back at our suite at noon if no one finds her," I said.

Viv and Andre nodded and headed for the stairs. I turned to Harry and said, "Are you thinking what I'm thinking?"

"We start in the library?" he asked.

I nodded. He took my hand and we strolled through the

magnificent castle, past tapestries and portraits and rooms filled with furniture that was centuries old. How many butts had sat in those seats over the years? It boggled.

When we reached the hallway that led to the library, I noticed a constable was standing in front of the door, which was closed.

"I think they're guarding it because it's a crime scene," I said. "What do we do?"

"Follow my lead," Harry said. He raised his free hand and greeted the constable. "Hi, we were told the library was down this passageway, but we haven't seen it. You don't happen to know where it is, do you?"

"Sure I do," the man said. He was middle-aged and his uniform looked like it had seen better days. I suspected he'd been on the job for most of his adult life. "It's in there." He hooked his thumb at the door behind him.

"Oh, thank you, that's convenient," Harry said. He began to walk around the constable to the door.

"Oy!" the constable shouted. "You can't go in there. I'm guarding it, yeah?"

"Oh." Harry looked confused. "Why?"

"Because there was a murder done in there," the constable said. "Or at least, that's where they found the dead guy."

"So no one is allowed inside?" I clarified. "Even if I just want to go in and pick out a book to read?"

"No, ma'am, I'm sorry," he said. "Detective Inspector's orders. The library is empty and Detective Stewart wants to keep it that way. I've been on duty for hours and no one has gone in."

"Or out?" Harry asked. "No one's come out of there either, right?"

"Of course not," the constable said. He looked annoyed. "I'm here, aren't I? I'd notice if someone came out of there, yeah?"

"Right, absolutely, sir. Sorry to have disturbed you," Harry said. He was using his placating tone, which when he turned it on me, made me want to kick him, but I could see how it settled the ruffled feathers of the constable.

"We'll just find something to read elsewhere," Harry said. He took me by the elbow and led me away.

"What are we going to do now?" I asked. "We have the entire first floor to cover, and the place I thought Sunny was most likely to be is locked up and guarded."

Harry glanced down at my feet. I was wearing trainers. Then he fingered my sweater as if to determine how thick it was. "I wish you had a jacket on," he said. "But we won't be in the tunnel long, so this will have to do."

"We're going to the outside entrance, aren't we?" I asked. My voice came out high and I cleared my throat. It wasn't that I was opposed to the idea, I just really didn't want to run into the murderer in a tunnel with only two exits.

"It's the only way we can get into the library," he said. "It might be for nothing if Detective Inspector Stewart stationed another constable in the garden, watching the tunnel exit. But if he didn't, then we can use it to sneak into the library and see if Sunny is in there."

"Wouldn't they have checked for her there?" I asked.

"Who knows?" he said. "If she discovered the tunnel,

she may have used it to get in there. She also might have used it to hide if they came into the library looking for her."

"Or she's living in there presently because she used the tunnel to kill Dooney, and now that everyone thinks she's pregnant with Dooney's child and had a reason to murder him, it's her permanent hideout."

"That's dark," he said. "Did she strike you as the sort of person who would do that?"

"Actually, no," I said. "She seemed very naive and sweet and a lot overwhelmed by everything that's happened to her."

"But if she is pregnant, she could have used the castle tunnel to sneak up on Dooney and bend him to her will," he said. "Make him back out of his wedding to Piper and marry her instead."

"Or she thought she could and when he refused, she murdered him," I said. I shook my head. I didn't know Sunny at all, but it just seemed so unlikely. Trisha was another story; that one had crime of passion written all over her. Even Piper seemed the sort who could resort to murder if pushed hard enough, but Sunny? No.

Harry led me outside and we strolled through the garden. We were trying to look casual until we were out of sight of the castle and then we jogged across the hillside to the hidden door. There was no one guarding it and Archie hadn't put a *Staff Only* sign on it yet, so I felt like entering the tunnel wasn't a flagrant violation of the castle rules.

I kept watch while Harry pulled the door wide. When

he waved me over, I scooted behind the trellis and followed him. He shut the door behind us and I flicked on the light switch. And there we were again, making our way back into the castle through the secret passageway.

"Should we call her name?" I whispered to Harry. "I wouldn't want to startle her."

"It might frighten her more if we do," he said. "Assuming she's in the tunnel, the idea of being discovered might scare her. I know you don't think she's the murderer but you have to consider the possibility, especially since she disappeared."

"Maybe she's just hiding because she's afraid that whoever killed Dooney is going to murder her, too," I said.

"That's a good theory," he agreed. "Either way, we need to find her for her own safety. It can't be healthy to be pregnant and hiding. She needs to be eating regular meals and resting."

The wall sconces didn't illuminate the entire tunnel. We passed from each circle of light, straining to see up ahead. I didn't see a person, and the truth was that I was less nervous in the tunnel this time. It helped that I knew we would end up in the library. I wondered if Archie would be there to chastise us again.

I really wished I could turn back time to that afternoon, when Dooney was obnoxious but not dead. Although, if I was being honest with myself, I would go all the way back to the day that Andre and I ran into Piper. I would never have convinced Viv to design the bridesmaids' hats.

"What are you thinking about?" Harry asked. "I can practically hear the wheels turning in your brain."

"Just that if I had it to do over, I would never have encouraged Viv to take this job," I said. "What a disaster."

"Not entirely," he said.

"What do you mean?"

"Well, you have managed to scratch 'castle' off your list of possible wedding venues," he said.

"There is that," I agreed. "Although I'm still partial to you in a kilt."

I heard him chuckle.

We reached the bottom of the stairs. There'd been no sign of Sunny in the tunnel. No heap of blankets or traces of food on the floor. If she had come this way, then she'd only used the tunnel as a passage and hadn't hidden in it.

"Well, this was a bust," I said.

"Not necessarily," Harry said. "Didn't you find her hiding in the library after Dooney was murdered?"

I nodded. "But I assumed she went through the door while Archie and I were gone."

"But she might have used the tunnel," he said. "If the library has been closed off like the constable said, she could be hiding in there."

"She did say she used the tunnel before. It's a good place to hide," I said. "I mean there's plenty to read, comfy chairs, and she has her own access point."

Harry nodded and whispered, "Let's go."

I followed him up the stairs, staying close to the wall. When he reached the door, the knob wouldn't budge. It was locked from the inside.

"Blast!" Harry said. "Now we know why no one is watching the tunnel exit. The door is locked. There's no access to the library this way."

I maneuvered around him and looked at the lock. I glanced at Harry. "Do you have a credit card?"

"Planning to do some shopping?" he asked.

I laughed. "No. When I was in the hotel industry, they taught us the different ways people could open locked doors, hoping we'd be better at spotting security risks. One of the ways was with a credit card and a lock that looks like this sort."

Harry lifted his eyebrows and took out his wallet. He fished out a card and handed it to me.

"Perfect." I knelt down again and shoved the card in between the door and the frame parallel with the knob. No luck. I pushed on the door a bit and *pop*, the door swung open.

"I don't know whether to be impressed or horrified," Harry said. "I'm leaning towards impressed."

I returned his somewhat mangled credit card. "Sorry."

"And the pendulum swings back to horrified," he said. He pocketed the card.

Harry put his arm in front of me, holding me in place, while he peeked around the edge of the open door to make sure it was clear. No one was waiting to clobber us with a fire poker, so that was a good sign.

He put his finger to his lips and stepped inside. I followed and closed the door behind me. The library was quiet, the ticking of the grandfather clock in the corner the only sound. I scanned the room. It was empty. My gaze went to the spot where I'd found Dooney's body. The carpet was pristine, there wasn't even a depression in the thick nap to show that a dead man had lain there. It was hard to believe that just two days ago, Dooney Portis had been murdered.

Harry gestured with his hand for us to move forward. I followed him. We walked across the room silently. We looked down the aisles between the short bookcases to see if anyone was hiding. There was no one. Disappointment weighed my shoulders down. I really thought we'd find Sunny here.

I did a visual sweep of the room just to be sure. I glanced at the chairs in front of the fireplace. They were empty. The settee faced away from us, and just to be thorough I walked around it. And there, curled up like a child, was Sunny fast asleep.

Chapter 14

I turned toward Harry, put my finger to my lips and pointed. He moved close enough to see her, and his eyes widened. He was as surprised as I was that we'd actually found her. I pantomimed that I would approach her and that he should stay out of sight. I didn't want to freak her out. He nodded. I waited while he moved to crouch behind one of the nearby freestanding bookcases. He was close enough to hear everything, and to help me if I needed it.

Tiptoeing so as not to make any noise, I approached the small couch. I don't know why it didn't occur to me earlier, but given that I had found Dooney in a similar position in this very room, it hit me suddenly that Sunny could be dead.

I sucked in a breath. I stared at her chest, trying to see if it was rising and falling. I couldn't tell. I felt woozy. If Sunny was . . . well, I didn't think I could handle that. But the possibility was very real. If Dooney was murdered because he'd had an affair with Sunny, then didn't it stand to reason that Sunny could be murdered for the same thing?

As I drew closer with dread in my heart, Sunny shifted. I jumped and almost yelped, but I managed to keep it in. Phew.

I squatted beside her so that I wasn't looming over her. I gently put my arm on her shoulder and said, "Sunny, you need to wake up."

She jumped, but mercifully didn't yelp. Instead she shoved back from me, pressing herself into the couch. Her eyes were huge and I knew she didn't recognize me.

"It's me, Scarlett, one of the hatmakers," I said. "Don't be scared. I'm not here to hurt you."

She put her hand on her heart and took several deep breaths.

"Are you all right?" I asked.

She nodded. She glanced at the main door, which was still shut. "How did you get in here?"

"The tunnel," I said.

"But I locked that door," she said.

"There are ways around that," I said. I decided to remain vague and see what she said.

"Credit card?" She nodded. "I did the same. I used to lose the keys to my flat all the time. It's a handy skill to have."

I had to agree.

"Sunny, why are you hiding in here?" I asked. "Isn't it . . ."

"Creepy to be in the room where he died?" she asked.

I nodded. I rose from my crouch and sat on the edge of a nearby chair.

"I feel closer to him when I'm here," she said. Her face crumpled and she sobbed. "This is all such a nightmare." She put a hand protectively on her belly.

"Sunny, is it true? Are you having Dooney's child?" I asked.

She hesitated. It was clear she didn't want to answer, but then she sighed and nodded. A tear spilled down over her cheek.

"I don't know how to ask my next question," I said.

"You want to know if I killed him because he was marrying Piper?" she asked.

"Yeah, I do," I said.

She shook her head. "No, I loved him. I could never have harmed him. He's the father of my child."

"Have you spoken to Detective Stewart?"

She shook her head. "I've been avoiding him. I know he thinks I did it. I'd think I did it, too, but I didn't. I swear I didn't." She paused and took a deep breath. "That's the other reason I've been hiding out in here when I'm not wandering the castle grounds, ducking the detective. While the officers were searching the library, I listened in on their conversations through the tunnel door to hear what they knew."

"That was a huge risk if you were discovered," I said.

"They make a lot of noise when they enter the library. Plenty of time for me to go hide in the tunnel." She shrugged. "Besides, judging by the lack of evidence found so far, the police can't prove anything. And really, what do I have to lose? I didn't murder Dooney and I have no idea how I'm going to prove that."

"I believe you," I said. I had no idea why I said that. I had no proof. She was the perfect suspect—she had motive and opportunity. I wasn't sure about means since the detective hadn't told us what exactly had killed Dooney. Still, there was no reason to think that she was innocent.

"I thought about trying to leave the castle," Sunny said. "I planned to go to Devon to stay with my mum. She didn't like Dooney. She told me he was going to go through with marrying Piper for her money and then forget all about me and the baby. She was wrong, but she loves me and I know she'll stand by us. But I can't leave until I know what happened."

I couldn't fault her. I'd feel exactly the same way.

"How did Trisha know about you and the baby?" I asked. "You two don't seem especially close."

"We're not," Sunny said. "I'm not friends with any of them, not really. A few weeks ago, we were at a house party in the Cotswolds, and Trisha overheard Dooney and I when we slipped out to be alone. We were talking about the baby and what to do, and she figured out that the baby was his. Dooney threatened to destroy her if she told anyone."

Given what Piper had said about Trisha being in love with Dooney, this made me wonder if Trisha could have been furious enough to kill Dooney not only for marrying Piper but for having a child with Sunny, as well. That must have felt like being rejected twice by him.

"If you're not close with the others, how did you become a bridesmaid?" I asked.

"Dooney suggested my name to Piper when she needed one more bridesmaid to keep the number even with the ushers. Dooney said he had a plan, that he just had to wait for the right time, and then he and I would run away together before the wedding ceremony."

"That seems like a sketchy plan," I said. "How did you fall in with this group anyway?"

"I knew Dooney when we were kids. My mother worked for his mother as a secretary back when they had money. Then Piper and I became acquainted when we worked together in London. She'd invite me along when she went out with her friends. I think she felt sorry for me, because I'm from a middle-class background. Trisha and the other bridesmaids are from some posh secondary school they all attended with Piper. It was clear from the start that I didn't fit into their world, but Trisha in particular was always very clear to point it out at every turn."

"I'm sorry," I said. "That must have stung."

"It did at first," she said. "Not that I care what any of them think of me. I never meant to fall for Dooney, you know, but he was the only one who was always kind to me, who never made me feel like an outsider or a charity case, and I appreciated it. I know everyone says he was horrible, but he was never like that with me."

"Have you talked to Piper?" I asked.

"No, I haven't seen anyone since I ran out last night," she said.

"You need to talk to Detective Stewart," I said. "It looks bad the way it is now."

"I'm afraid he'll arrest me," she said. "And when Piper finds out that the baby is Dooney's, she's going to come after me. The Mays have a lot of money. They'll do everything they can to make it look like I did it."

"But if the evidence doesn't hold up, it doesn't matter how much money they have," I said. "The real killer will be caught but the police need to remove you as a suspect so that can happen."

She shook her head at me. "You know better than that. There are two sets of rules out there. One for people with money and one for the rest of us."

She wasn't wrong. I knew that, but she couldn't hide in the castle indefinitely.

"Even if the police do take you in for questioning, don't you think you'd be safer with them than alone in a castle with a murderer on the loose?" I asked. "If you're not worried about yourself, what about the baby? We have no idea who murdered Dooney or why or what lengths they'll go to in order to protect themselves."

She stared at me and then she nodded. "Maybe. But what if it wasn't a person that murdered him, or at least someone who's not a person anymore?"

"What do you mean?"

"You have to have heard the rumors," she said. "The McKenna bride and her curse."

"I don't think—" I began but she interrupted.

"But it happened before," she said. "I've heard the stories. Three times, brides who were to be married in the castle died just before the ceremony."

"The castle is over a thousand years old," I argued. "Of course people have died."

"But these were brides who didn't want to get married, just like the McKenna bride."

"I think those stories are coincidences that happen to fit the narrative of a ghost story," I said. "You know, to give the castle more allure to tourists and such."

"But what if it's true?" she insisted. "Then it's my fault Dooney is dead. Because he loved me and not the woman he was supposed to marry, the curse killed him."

"Listen to me very carefully," I said. "A curse didn't murder him. A person did and you could be next. Do you understand?"

She nodded. Her hair hung about her face. I noticed she was wearing the same clothes she'd been in at the dinner party, and she smelled like she could really use a bath.

"Why are you helping me?" she asked.

"Because I don't think you killed him," I said. "And because I know what it's like to be the outsider. Come on, let's get you cleaned up and we'll go find Detective Stewart."

Just then I heard the key in the lock of the library door. Harry popped up from between his shelves and hissed, "Someone's coming!"

Harry's sudden appearance made Sunny yelp, which I was certain could be heard from the door. Sunny shot up from the settee and dashed behind it as if she feared Harry was some sort of maniac there to kill her.

"It's okay, he's with me," I said. I tried to grab her hand but she backed away.

"Go!" she said. She waved her hands in the direction of the tunnel.

The doorknob started to turn and Harry grabbed my hand and pulled me across the library to the tunnel door. We dashed through, closing it almost all the way just as Detective Stewart swooped in and grabbed Sunny.

"Gotcha!"

I supposed we could have gone back inside the library, but how would that help Sunny? It wouldn't. Harry put a finger to my lips, clearly having come to the same conclusion.

"I've been looking for you, Ms. Bright," Detective Stewart said. "I have a lot of questions."

"Are you going to arrest me?" she asked.

"Did you murder Dooney Portis?"

"No!" she cried. I peeked through the tiny sliver of an opening in the door and watched. Sunny looked stricken, and it seemed to soften the detective just a little bit.

"If that's true," he paused, "then I won't arrest you."

He looked around the library and asked. "How did you get in here?"

"The door," she said.

She didn't say which door. She knew Harry and I were hiding in the tunnel, and she was covering for us. If Detective Stewart found us, I had no idea how we'd explain our presence in a way that would sound even remotely reasonable.

"Why have you been hiding?" he asked.

"Because there's a murderer in the castle and I'm afraid they might kill me or my baby," she said.

Good answer! No one could fault the lover of a murdered man who was also pregnant with his child for being afraid for the safety of her baby, especially when he was about to marry someone else. Wait, that didn't sound good for Sunny. Mercy, this was complicated.

Detective Stewart scratched his chin. "Or you're hiding in here because you murdered Dooney Portis and you're afraid of being caught."

"I didn't," she cried. "I didn't do it. I would never. He was the father of my child."

"He was also about to marry someone else," Detective Stewart said. "That's quite a motive to murder him."

"I didn't," Sunny said. Her voice was soft.

I pushed closer to the door, wanting to intercede, but Harry wrapped his arm around me and kept me back. He was right. I could only imagine what Detective Stewart would think if we popped out at him. It was so frustrating.

"I'll need you to come with me," Detective Stewart said. "I have an office in the village where I can interview you properly."

Sunny glanced furtively in our direction. I didn't know if it was because she was pondering her escape or looking to see if we were listening. As soon as the door shut behind them, Harry closed the door and led me down the stairs.

"We have to help her," I said.

"Ginger, what if she is the murderer?" he asked.

"She isn't," I said.

"How do you know?"

"I just do," I said.

"Not exactly something that would hold up in a court of law," he said.

"I know," I said. "But she's not like the others. She's . . . nice."

"Doesn't mean she's not a murderer."

"I know," I said.

"But you still believe she's innocent."

"I do," I said. My voice was soft when I said, "I know what it's like to be lied to, to be mocked and derided when you put your trust in the wrong person."

"All the more reason for her to have wanted to murder him," he said.

"Unless he was telling her the truth," I countered. "Maybe he was planning to duck out of the wedding and run away with her."

"Then that would make Piper the most likely suspect as the jilted bride," he said.

"Or Trisha, the bridesmaid who has loved him from afar, and was clearly jealous of his relationship with Sunny," I said.

"Or the Mays if they got wind of his plan to abandon their daughter," Harry said.

"I feel like we're on a poorly written reality show," I said.

"Agreed. We also need to find out whom we overheard arguing in the garden when we first arrived," he said. "It could have been Dooney and his killer."

"What can we do to help Sunny right now?" I asked.

"I'll call Alistair," he said. "He should be able to recommend someone to represent her if she needs it."

"Thank you," I said.

When we reached the door that led to the garden, Harry insisted on going first. He opened the door and peered out, making sure there was no one about, before opening it wide. I snapped off the tunnel's lights before we went on our way.

Viv sent me a text that they had finished searching their floors and were back in the suite waiting for us. When we arrived, she and Andre were enjoying lunch while discussing what they'd seen in the castle.

"Well?" Viv asked when we entered. "How is Sunny? Your text was very lacking in detail."

"She's scared," I said. "It turns out the baby is Dooney's."

Viv gasped and Andre blinked. They took a moment to take it in.

"Well, that's a game changer," Andre said. "Where did you find her?"

"The library," Harry answered.

Both Viv and Andre looked behind us, expecting Sunny to be there, no doubt.

"Small problem," I said. I took a seat at the table and Harry did, too. "Detective Stewart arrived just after we did and took Sunny to his office for questioning."

"Not great," Andre said.

"I've called Alistair," Harry said.

"Oh, is he coming?" Viv asked. She sounded excited and then caught herself and became more composed. "Because that would be fine."

Harry's lips twitched just a bit before he said, "No, he can't leave London but he has a friend in the area who can help."

"Oh." Viv sounded disappointed, which I understood completely. She and Alistair had been dating for a while now but she was new at the whole relationship thing, having made nothing but poor choices previously. I wasn't judging her. I, too, chose poorly before I met Harry.

"What happens now?" Andre asked.

"The only way we can help Sunny is to find out who killed Dooney," I said.

"No, nope, absolutely not," Andre said. "I was fine with looking for Sunny, because a young woman shouldn't be roaming around a castle when there's a murderer loose. But I do not want to go looking for the murderer myself."

"He has a point," Viv said. "I mean, isn't that why Detective Stewart is here?"

"Yes, but he doesn't have access to everyone the way we do," I said. "We can mix and mingle with the guests and use Viv's celebrity to get them talking about hats and then segue into Dooney's murder."

"Because that's a natural conversational trajectory," Andre said. "'Like my hat? Seen any murders lately?' Not suspicious at all."

I gave him a reproving look and he shrugged. "I'm not saying that we have to risk our lives. I'm just saying that since we're stuck here for at least another twenty-four hours, we should try and figure out what happened to Dooney and if that helps Sunny, all the better."

"Ginger and I were discussing possible suspects on our

way here, and I think we should start with the bridal party," Harry said. "Trisha was clearly disturbed by the marriage, and now that Sunny has admitted that the baby is Dooney's, that gives Piper a motive, too."

Viv raised one eyebrow. "You might have dated a murderer, Harrison."

He winced. "Which we will never discuss again if it proves to be true."

I patted his shoulder. "At least it was only two dates."

"When Dooney came by here right after we arrived," I said to Viv, "do you remember how smug he was?"

"That's his default setting," she said.

"Doesn't it strike you as odd that he was behaving like that?" I asked. "Sunny said they were planning to run away together, that he was going to duck out of the wedding and jilt Piper at the altar."

"Rude," Viv said.

"But if that was the case, why was he so pleased with himself when he was here?" I asked. "He kept talking about his fortunes turning around, that this wedding was the best thing that had ever happened to him, and that he'd never have to work again."

"I remember," Viv said. "I assumed that he was just reveling in the windfall of money he would get when he married Piper and achieved her family's dream of belonging in the rarefied air of the upper class."

"I did, too," I said. "But what if he didn't mean that?"

"What else could he have meant?" Harry asked. "Sunny has a promising career but nothing like the money he'd be seeing if he married Piper."

"We still don't know who he was talking to in the garden," I said. "Maybe Dooney was murdered not because he cheated on Piper but because she found out he was going to leave her at the altar."

"Would he have been demanding money from her to not leave her at the altar?" I asked. "Or maybe, he was demanding it from her family?"

"I only know Matthew May by reputation in the financial world," Harry said. His expression grew serious. "I would never, ever cross him."

"I'm beginning to prefer the idea that a curse took Dooney out," Andre said.

"Hard to prove, though," I said. I glanced at the time on my phone. "The wedding was supposed to happen a few hours from now. Any idea if they've planned anything in its place?"

"Like what?" Viv asked.

"I don't know," I said. "A wake for Dooney? A service? A gathering? Anything?"

"Not that I've heard, but I can go to her room and ask Piper," Viv said. "One concerned friend to another."

"Perfect," I said. "Come on, Harry. There are more spots in the castle I want to check out."

My intended had just started eating a pasty and shook his head. "I don't know what you're thinking, but we eat first." He pointed to my empty plate with his fork.

"But there's a murderer roaming the halls," I protested.

"And we won't be able to fight them off if we're starving," he said. He pointed again at my empty plate.

"Fine." How the man could be hungry when there was

a mystery to be solved and lives to be saved, I had no idea. I lifted one of the pasties onto my plate and stabbed it with my fork. I took a bite and—oh, my. It was so good. They'd stuffed the delicate pie pastry with rosemary-seasoned chicken and chunks of potatoes. I thought I might swoon.

"I told you so," Harry said.

I waved my fork at him. Whatever.

"I'll go visit Piper," Viv said. She glanced at Andre. "Will you be okay by yourself? I know you were about to go take more pictures."

"Me? Of course, why wouldn't I be?"

We were all silent and he rolled his eyes.

"Ghosts don't come out in daylight," he said. He paused and added, "Right?"

"Absolutely," I said. "Strictly a nighttime thing."

"One hundred percent," Harry said.

Andre visibly relaxed in his seat. "I suppose I'll go take pictures then. Meet you all back here?"

"Definitely," I agreed. "Keep your phones with you, in case something happens."

I didn't say what might happen. I didn't need to. There was a murderer among the guests and "something" was definitely code for another murder.

Viv left and Andre followed soon after with his camera. When Harry and I finished our meal, he asked, "All right, where did you want to go?"

"The veranda," I said. "There was a lot happening right before I found Dooney in the library, and I want to see if I can remember anything suspicious."

"Solid plan," he said. "Let's go."

There were more guests moving around the castle today. Mercifully, I did not run into the May cousins from Yorkshire. If the salty one had placed me as the party crasher, I didn't want to have to explain myself.

We arrived on the veranda. The sun was warm and the breeze was light and cool. The gardens were bursting with blooms. It was a picture-perfect day for a wedding. Poor Piper. I had no idea how she was going to come back from this.

"Describe the evening to me," Harry said.

So, I did. I pointed to where different people had been standing, the music, the bars, the atmosphere of celebration. I mentioned that Dooney and his best man, Quentin, had disappeared from view and were smoking at the bottom of the terrace steps behind the bushes. Piper had seen them sneak off and looked furious with Dooney. According to Viv, he'd promised Piper he'd quit.

Harry nodded. "That description fits. Piper could always be very exacting in getting what she wanted."

"If Dooney died in the library shortly after being here, then doesn't it stand to reason that he was poisoned at the cocktail party?" he said. "You said there were no marks on him, so that would leave poison as the most obvious cause of death. And with a crowded bar who knows how many people had access to his drinks?"

"Bartenders, waitstaff, anyone who brought him a drink," I said. "Meaning anyone who was at the party is a suspect." I groaned.

"Which would be why Detective Stewart is keeping you all here," Harry said.

"We're getting nowhere." I tapped my chin with my forefinger. "I remember that Dooney and Quentin, his best man, were at the bar, and Dooney was being rude to the bartender."

"His usual self then," Harry observed. "Sorry, shouldn't speak ill of the dead and all that."

"No, but his off-putting personality could be the cause of his murder," I said. "So, it's a factor to consider. Perhaps the murderer is just someone who was tired of him."

"What was Dooney's relationship with his best man like?" he asked.

"That is an excellent question, and I wish we could ask Sunny," I said. There was nothing left to see on the veranda. "Why do you suppose Dooney was in the library? He didn't strike me as a big reader."

"Could be that he started to feel poorly," Harry said. "And, like you, maybe he couldn't find the loo."

"Let's walk over there," I said. "Maybe we'll get an idea on the way."

We left the veranda and cut through the dining room. There were no staff or guests buzzing around. I was grateful for the quiet because it made it easier to think.

"So, we're Dooney," I said. Harry made a face, but I ignored him. "We've been poisoned and we feel wretched."

"He'd likely want to find a place to either be sick or lie down," Harry said.

"But I found him in the library while I was looking for

the washroom, so he could have made the same error I did. Or maybe he went into the library to lie down?"

"But never made it to the couch, and collapsed on the floor."

"Exactly."

I was beginning to learn my way around the castle and was pleased that I made only one wrong turn—Harry corrected me—on our way to the library. The door was open just a few inches and there was no constable in sight. Huh. Had they stopped guarding it then?

Harry and I were about to cross the hall and enter the room, when the door opened wider. Harry pulled me to the side into an alcove that was framed with heavy brocade drapes. We pressed ourselves against the wall, trying to stay out of sight behind the fabric.

Chapter 15

"How can you not have found it? You've had days."

"Beg pardon, ma'am, but the detective has kept this room locked and guarded until today when they found Miss Bright in here and decided they'd collected all the evidence possible. I've barely had any time at all to search."

I'd know that brogue anywhere. I inched forward to confirm. It was indeed Archie Carlton, but who was he talking to? I caught sight of the other person's back and recognized Rita May, of the hourglass figure and long dark hair.

"Well, I'm not paying you to do nothing," Rita snapped. "Find it."

Harry and I pressed back against the wall as she stormed

away. Archie heaved a heavy sigh and returned to the library.

"What do you suppose that was all about?" I whispered.

"No idea, but whatever she's paying him to look for, it's in the library," Harry replied. "Let's see if we can find out."

As soon as Rita disappeared around the corner, Harry led the way out of the alcove and through the open door. Archie was muttering to himself as he stood in front of the floor-to-ceiling bookcases that lined the walls. He was clearly looking for something as he pulled books down, thumbed through them and put them back. He crouched down to examine one of the lower shelves, leaning in to select a book.

"What are you looking for, Archie?" I asked.

He shot up, cracked his head on the bookshelf above him and clapped his hand to the wound.

"What's the idea, eh? You scared me half to death and made me smack my head," he grumbled.

"What is Rita May paying you to look for?" Harry asked.

Personally, I thought it was too soon to ask that question. I'd been planning to finesse Archie a little before we jumped right to it.

"I don't know what you're talking about," he balked.

"We overheard you talking, Archie," I said. "What is it that Mrs. May is missing?"

"Em . . . an earring," Archie said. He didn't look at us

when he spoke. Instead he was studying the ground at his feet. "She lost it during the . . . um . . ."

"Murder," I said.

"Yeah . . . wait . . . no!" He glared at me. "Don't try to put words in my mouth."

I raised my hands in the air as if in surrender. "Sorry, it just seemed odd, given that her future son-in-law was found dead in this room that she thought she might have lost an earring in here as well."

Archie looked uncomfortable. "Well, there was a lot of comings and goings after he was found, and she was in here consoling her daughter. It easily could have fallen off."

"Uh-huh," Harry said. "Does Detective Stewart know you're helping her?"

"No, why would I tell him? I'm just trying to be a good caretaker," Archie said. "I don't think there's any need to get the detective all riled up. Besides, the earring is probably in her room and she just misplaced it. No reason to get everyone in an uproar. I'm just humoring her."

"So, you won't be taking any money from her, because if you're just humoring her, that doesn't warrant getting paid, correct?" Harry asked.

Archie's shoulders slumped in defeat. "I have to go make my rounds." He stomped out the door without another word.

"Well, this is an interesting turn of events," Harry said.

"I'll say," I agreed. I walked to the shelf that Archie had been examining. "I don't believe that nonsense about a missing earring for a hot second."

"Me either," he said. He moved to stand beside me and we stared at the shelf together. "Do you think she's missing a book?"

I shrugged. "The bigger question is, Does all this have anything to do with Dooney's murder, or is it just coincidental?"

"I don't believe anything is coincidental during a murder investigation," he said.

"Right," I said. "Should we look around then?"

"Why not?" he asked. "Maybe we'll stumble upon the item, whatever it is."

Harry and I spent a half hour checking the shelves and perusing the books. Honestly, I could have spent all afternoon there, but there was nothing that stood out as unusual. We left the library, closing the door behind us.

We were halfway down the hallway when Piper turned into the corridor from another room. A parlor by the looks of it. She had a stack of magazines in her arms and was headed for the library.

"Piper, hi," I said.

"Hi." She glanced at us and a faint smile curved her lips. Her voice was low and soft as if she didn't have the energy to put much effort into it.

"Is there anything we can do for you?" I asked. I knew I was overstepping but I couldn't seem to help myself. Despite the fact that Dooney had been cheating on her, I just found it hard to believe that she would have killed Dooney and blown up her entire life.

"No, but thank you." She looked at Harry when she

said it, as if I weren't even there. I told myself they went way back and I shouldn't be annoyed, but still.

"We just ran into your mother in the library," Harry said. "She and Archie, the caretaker, were looking for a missing earring of hers."

Piper's eyebrows rose. "Really? An earring? In the library?" Somehow she made it sound suspicious. Hmm.

"Yes," I said. I felt the need to insert myself into the conversation. "She didn't mention it to you?"

"No." Piper shook her head. "I'm certain it will turn up."

"Maybe you'll find it," Harry said.

"Perhaps. If you'll excuse me." Piper gestured to her magazines and we both nodded.

"Of course, sorry to hold you up," Harry said. He took my arm and we moved aside to let her pass. "We'll see you later."

As soon as she was out of hearing range, I said, "That was the most awkward conversation I've ever had."

"Painful even," he said.

"Do you think it's because we mentioned her mother?" I asked.

"Maybe, but I don't see why," he said. "I think it's the natural weirdness of what this weekend was supposed to be and what it's become."

"Good point," I said. "How could anything be normal under the circumstances?"

We climbed the stairs, hoping that Viv had more luck during her visit with Piper than we did. Despite the number of miles I walked with Bella every day, the castle stairs still left me a bit winded. I paused at the top and motioned for Harry to wait while I caught my breath.

He leaned against the wall beside the door to one of the salons and checked his phone for messages. I heard a faint giggle and glanced at Harry, wondering if he had heard the same thing. Harry looked up at me and put his finger over his lips. He pointed to the door beside him. It was open just a smidge and we peeked inside, with me crouching low and Harry leaning over me.

It was Quentin, the best man, and Trisha, the angry bridesmaid. They were sprawled on the furniture, which was upholstered in a deep rich red. A bottle of wine and a half-full glass were in front of Trisha, while an expensive bottle of Macallan whiskey sat beside Quentin, who was smoking.

I was quite certain the castle had a no-smoking policy inside, with a designated outside area for smokers, but I let it go. I wanted to hear what they said while they commenced day drinking.

Trisha giggled again at something Quentin muttered. His voice was slurred. It was clear that he was drunk. I couldn't really fault him, given that his best friend was dead. If it were me, I'd be drunk, too.

"How rich are you, Trisha the fair?" Quentin asked.

"It's vulgar to ask about a person's finances," she said. She reached for her glass, sipped her drink and then laughed. "But to answer your question, you could never afford me."

"Because I'm as poor as Dooney was?" he asked. "You didn't seem to mind that he was broke."

"That's because Dooney's family is still high society and he offers a girl status, which has a price beyond measure," she said.

"Piper May is going to have to lower her standards then," he said. He drained his drink and dropped his cigarette into the empty glass, letting the remaining ice cubes put it out.

Trisha went very still. "What do you mean?"

"Dooney let me in on a little moneymaking scheme of his before he died," Quentin said. "And since I no longer have my best friend to look after me, I'm going to use his secret to make myself rich."

I squeezed Harry's hand, trying to signal that I was freaking out. He squeezed back. Was this a confession? Had Quentin murdered his best friend because of the secret Dooney had shared?

"How rich?" Trisha asked.

"Come here and I'll tell you," Quentin said. He patted the sofa cushion beside him invitingly.

Ew. At that, I wanted to leave but I didn't want to miss a confession if one was forthcoming.

With a giggle, Trisha pushed up from her chair and wobbled her way around the table to plop down beside him. Her wine splashed with the momentum and Quentin scooped it out of her hand and set it on the table.

She pushed his shoulder. "Tell me."

He leaned back against the couch and crooked his finger, gesturing for her to come closer. I had a sudden vision of Little Red Riding Hood and the Big Bad Wolf, although honestly Trisha was about as far from an innocent young woman as a person could get.

She laughed and shimmied closer. He waved her in until she was almost in his lap, then he grabbed her about the waist and pushed her down onto the sofa so he could lean over her. I felt Harry stiffen beside me. I knew he would kick in the door if he thought Trisha was being taken advantage of, and I was right there with him.

Instead, she let out a throaty sexy laugh. They proceeded to kiss and Quentin whispered seemingly lewd suggestions in her ear.

Okay, that was enough! Whatever he was about to tell her had obviously been pushed aside in favor of their mutual lust.

Harry and I backed away as one. We hurried farther down the hallway a bit before we spoke.

"Gross," I said. "I think I need a shower."

"Right," he said. "And perhaps some bleach for my eyes."

I laughed. "That's what we get for eavesdropping."

"I really thought we were on the brink of hearing a confession," he said. "I mean, if Dooney had a money-making scheme and he told his best friend, who is also broke, then it stands to reason his best friend might have been the one to murder him."

"I had the same thought," I said. "Otherwise, I would never have lingered there."

"Yes, because as you said—gross," he agreed.

We walked along the corridor until we turned down the hallway to our room. We had just passed the first door when the sound of a scream ripped through the quiet like a siren blast. Harry and I both jumped and turned to face each other.

"Where did that come from?" I asked. My heart sank, fearing he was going to affirm what I was thinking.

"The parlor where we saw Quentin and Trisha," he said. "Come on."

We ran back down the hall. Other guests popped out of their rooms and followed us as we hurried by. The door was still open just a bit and Harry shoved it wide. Trisha was trapped under the inert weight of Quentin. She was pushing at him and screaming.

"Something's wrong with him. Get him off me!" she cried. She was wriggling beneath Quentin, who was completely slack.

"Trisha, stop!" I said. "We need to lift him off you."

"Hurry! I can't breathe," she cried. She began to sob.

Harry and I stepped forward, but one of the male guests nudged me aside to help Harry lift Quentin off Trisha. As soon as they got him up, Trisha scrambled over the arm of the couch and stood, righting her clothing and fluffing her hair.

"What's going on in here?" Piper May came charging into the room with Detective Stewart beside her.

"He's not breathing," Harry said. He looked at the detective. "We need an ambulance. Now!"

One of the constables appeared and at the detective's order, he ushered everyone out of the room. Harry and I were the last to leave while Trisha was detained by the detective since she was with Quentin when he blacked out or fainted or whatever was happening.

Harry and I stood in the hallway with the others. Viv and Andre appeared, and Harry told them what had happened.

"To be clear," Viv said. "The two of them were . . . and then he . . ."

"Yes," I said.

"Well, that's sorted," Andre said. He raised his hands in the air in exasperation. "Details, spell it out please."

I was about to explain in greater detail when a constable stepped out of the red salon, closing the door behind him. Questions were fired at him by the guests in the hallway, and he held up his hands in a gesture to be quiet.

"Everyone is to go to their rooms. Keep your doors locked, and await further instructions," he said. "Detective Inspector Stewart will be visiting each of your rooms to interview you personally."

"Is he dead?" Piper asked.

A couple of medics appeared, taking the stairs two at a time. The officer gestured for them to go into the room. I glanced inside when the door opened, and Quentin was still on the floor, where Harry and the other man had put him. That didn't bode well.

"I'm not at liberty to answer any questions at this time," the constable said. He made a shooing gesture with his hands and the crowd started to disperse.

Harry and I followed Viv and Andre back to our suite. I leaned close to Harry and asked, "Do you think he was murdered, too?"

"Two men in their prime, both dying so quickly like that?" he asked. "Yeah, I think he was murdered, too."

A chill rippled through me. "Well, at least we know it wasn't the curse, because Quentin wasn't about to marry anyone."

"That is not as reassuring as you'd think," Andre said.

Viv opened the door and we filed into the room, which, despite its opulence, I was beginning to loathe.

Chapter 16

"You don't think the detective is going to demand that we stay here even longer while they investigate what happened to Quentin, do you?" Viv asked. She sank onto the divan, looking as if she just couldn't bear it.

"I don't know," Harry said. "But I'd doubt it. Everyone here has a life they have to get back to tomorrow."

I nodded. "I don't think I've ever wanted to go home so badly in my life."

"All right, you two, since we have time to kill, what is the plan for your wedding?" Viv asked. "I know everything was shut down during the pandemic and you had to postpone it, but don't you think it's time you committed to a date, a color scheme, a venue or anything?"

Harry and I looked at each other. It was true. We were

supposed to get married ages ago but then the world went sideways and we decided to wait since my family was in the United States and they couldn't come. I'd had big plans and dreams and hopes for my wedding but now after this weekend, I realized I didn't care what our wedding looked like.

"So long as I'm Mrs. Harry Wentworth and you're Mr. Scarlett Parker at the end of the day, I do not care about the wedding at all," I said.

Harry grinned at me. "I feel exactly the same."

Viv jumped up from her seat and said, "Yes! Set a date right now."

I would have protested but Andre chimed in. "She's right. Do it. Do it right now."

Harry took out his phone and opened the calendar app. "Do you think we could pull this off in six months?"

"Absolutely," I said. Obviously, feeling way overconfident. "Let's get married in January of next year."

"Done," Harry said. He pulled me close and kissed me.

As always whenever Harry was in my orbit, I lost track of everything that was going on around me. When we broke apart, Andre had his camera out and Viv was smiling and nodding at the display screen.

She tapped the screen. "That's your save-the-date picture."

Andre turned the display to us. I gasped. It looked like something out of a movie. Harry and I were staring into each other's eyes, centered perfectly in the arched castle window with the rolling green hills in the background.

"Perfect," Harry said.

"Meant to be," I agreed.

A knock on the door interrupted the moment.

Viv crossed the room and pulled the door open. It was Detective Inspector Stewart. He looked past Viv at me and said, "Ms. Parker, you have an uncanny knack for being present when dead bodies are found."

I felt my stomach drop. "Quentin is dead?"

"Yes, and according to several witnesses, including the unfortunate young woman who was with the deceased, you two were the first on the scene." Detective Stewart's jaw was tight. He looked frustrated and furious. "I'd like to know how that happened?"

I have to say, it was refreshing to not be the only one in the hot seat. Having Harry by my side meant it wasn't just me in trouble anymore, and I really appreciated that.

"Wrong place, wrong time," Harry said.

Detective Stewart's eyes narrowed. "Tell me everything."

I glanced at Harry and he nodded, so I told the detective about being on the veranda and wondering what had caused Dooney's death. I told him we decided to retrace my steps to the library while I'd been looking for the bathroom and how we wondered if Dooney had been doing the same thing.

He seemed singularly unimpressed and could barely hide his impatience. I wanted to point out that he was the one who'd asked, but I suspected that wouldn't go well, so I held my retort in check and continued.

"Before we could go into the library, however, Rita May came out and she was having words with Archie Carlton."

Detective Stewart straightened up and his gaze sharpened. "What sort of words?"

"From what we could tell, she'd asked him to look for something that she'd lost in the library and she was very upset that he hadn't been able to find it," I said.

"What was it?"

"When we asked him, Archie said it was an earring," I said. "But I felt like he was prevaricating. He seemed very uncomfortable."

The detective's eyebrows rose. He turned to Harrison. "Anything to add?"

"No, that about covers it," he said. By silent agreement, he took over the telling of the story. "When we were headed back to our room, we happened upon the salon where the bridesmaid Trisha was enjoying drinks with the best man, Quentin."

"Were they the only two people in the room?"

Harry nodded. "He was telling her that Dooney let him in on a secret that was going to make him a lot of money."

"What secret?"

Harry looked uncomfortable and said, "We were just passing by and happened to catch that part of the conversation. They were . . . er . . . busy, so we moved along. We had almost arrived here at our room when we heard Trisha scream."

"And you knew that's who it was?" The detective's gaze was uncompromising.

"We just followed the noise." Harry shrugged. "And that's where it led."

The detective looked at me. "Anything to add?"

I shook my head.

"All right." Detective Stewart put his hands on his hips. "I don't know who you two think you are, but this is a formal police inquiry. You have insinuated yourselves into my case, jeopardizing our investigation, and I won't have it. The metropolitan police in London might invite you in, but here in Sussex, we do not. Am I clear?"

Harry opened his mouth to protest but I grabbed his hand and gave it a quick squeeze. As a people pleaser, I was the one who made certain all of our hat shop customers were satisfied, just as I used to do with my hotel guests during my hospitality career. There was no need to antagonize Detective Stewart. It would get us nowhere fast.

"Yes, sir," I said. "Absolutely. We meant no disrespect. We've just had an awful lot of time on our hands."

"Might I suggest you take up knitting," the detective growled. With that, he turned on his heel and strode out the door.

"Well," I said.

"Indeed," Viv added.

Harry's phone chimed and he glanced at it. He frowned. "It's work. I have to take it."

"Go ahead," I said. "You can use our room and I'll stay here with Viv and Andre."

"Thanks." He kissed me quick and then said to Viv, "Keep an eye on her."

"Of course," Viv said.

Harry left, closing the door behind him.

"I'm going to call Nick. I need him to talk me down," Andre said. "I swear my nerves are shot."

He went into his room and shut the door. Viv and I exchanged a glance. I was about to suggest we go for a walk in the garden, when there was another knock on our door.

"You don't think it's Detective Stewart coming back to yell at me some more, do you?" I asked.

"He was having a bit of a wobble," she said, which made me smile. "I'm sure he won't yell again."

Since I was closer, I crossed the room and opened the door. Standing outside was Dominick Falco.

"Hi, Dominick," I said. "Come in. Viv, look who's here."

"Dominick, what brings you by?" Viv rose from her seat and crossed the room. She held out her hand and tugged him gently inside. He pulled a large leather suitcase on wheels behind him.

"I heard in the village that you still weren't allowed to leave, and I thought to myself that by now, you must be bored beyond reason."

"I am," she cried. "I have nothing to do other than sketch ideas and I feel restless and mean."

He laughed. "I understand completely, which is why I brought some materials for you to play with."

"You did?" Viv's face lit up as if he'd offered her a five-pound chocolate bar. Well, that's what I'd look like if someone offered me a chocolate bar that big.

He rested the suitcase on the low table by the divan and popped the latches. When he opened it, a profusion of colors and cloths exploded out of the case.

"I thought we could spend some time discussing ideas that I've been toying with," he said.

Viv clasped her hands under her chin. "Oh, that would be amazing! Scarlett, you don't mind if we take over the room, do you?"

"Not at all," I said. "I can go read in your room or something."

She had already turned away and was examining the treasures Dominick had brought. Okay then.

I glanced out the window and noted that the afternoon sun was high. I was in a bored funk and thought it might be good to let the fresh air blow my bad mood away.

"I'm going for a walk in the garden," I called to Viv. She waved at me, which I took to mean *go*, so I did.

One of the things I loved most about England were the gardens. They were lush and green and ripe with blossoms. As I walked along the gravel path that led through the beds, I marveled at the sheer beauty surrounding me. I took a deep breath in and slowly exhaled. My shoulders dropped from around my ears as the tension I'd been carrying around since finding Quentin eased. That was, until I thought about Quentin and then they shot right back up.

I had no doubt that whoever had murdered Dooney had killed Quentin, too. But who and why? It had to be because of the secret that Dooney had shared with Quentin. It was too coincidental not to be the case. It was a secret that Dooney said was going to make him a lot of money. But why did he need money if he was marrying money? My head spun around and around, trying to figure out how the wedding of the year had turned into a double homicide.

I wandered into the maze. It was a magnificent sculpted yew creation that was six feet in height and covered a large portion of the garden with twists and turns and dead ends. Truly, it was brilliant. I didn't go in very far, just a few steps to get the feel of the maze. It towered over me and I imagined if I were a child how much fun I could have playing hide-and-seek inside of it.

I heard a whistling sound and the crunch of branches to my left. I turned and saw the deadly curved point of a scythe sticking through the bushes right beside me. I jumped and stepped back, going farther into the maze. Was one of the gardeners working on the hedge?

"Hello, person over here," I cried.

The scythe disappeared and I waited for the person to yell "sorry." They didn't. Instead, the blade appeared again, slicing angrily through the hedge, much, much too close to me for comfort.

"Hey!" I yelled. And then it hit me that this was on purpose. This person was actually trying to slice me in half like a big avocado. I didn't pause to think. I ran.

Here's the thing about panic running—it never goes well, especially when you're scared out of your mind. I ran to the right, then took a left, another left, and kept going into the maze thinking that they'd have a hard time finding me the deeper I went. I also hoped that there was another exit. I definitely didn't want to run out the way I came in and have them lop my head off in the process.

The mere thought of that had me doubling my speed, and I ran until I reached a dead end.

I am not a runner. I am not even a fast walker. I was doubled over, sucking air through my mouth, trying to get my lungs to reinflate. I was also trying to do it quietly in case the person had followed me and was even now creeping up on me. I staggered back the way I had come. I didn't want to be trapped in a dead end. The hedge was thick enough that there was no way I could jump over it or plow through it.

I came around a corner and there were two people standing there. I screamed. They screamed. As I was about to turn around and run, Andre yelled, "Scarlett, it's us. Me and Nick."

I spun back around. It was them. I took two steps forward and launched myself at them, grabbing them both around the neck and hugging them tight.

"Oh, man, you guys, there was this scythe and it came through the hedge and I think someone is trying to kill me," I panted.

They hugged me back and then Nick set me back on my feet and studied my face. "Sweetie, are you all right? You sound a teeny bit hysterical."

"Someone tried to kill me," I said. I gestured to the hedge. "A big old scythe came through and . . . I sound demented, don't I?"

"A touch," Andre said. Although he looked sympathetic.

I looked at Nick. "What are you doing here?"

"Andre told me that Harrison came down and I thought

that sounded like fun, so I decided that after seeing my last patient of the day, I would go for a drive in the country, too."

"Andre told you he's afraid of the ghost, didn't he?"

"I am not—" Andre began but Nick interrupted.

"Yes, he's been a nervous wreck since you arrived and he heard about it," Nick said.

"Well, you have to admit that Dooney's death could have been the curse," Andre said.

"Not anymore," I pointed out. "Quentin's death had nothing to do with the curse."

"That we know of," Andre said.

Nick and I exchanged a glance.

"Whoever just tried to give me a haircut with a scythe was not a ghost," I said.

Nick put his arm around me in a comforting half hug. "Come on, love, let's go get you some tea. I think this whole thing has caused you to imagine—"

Whoosh! The blade of the scythe appeared in the hedge right between us.

"Ah!" Nick yelled. He pushed Andre away from the hedge, grabbed my hand and started running. We turned left, then right, and then the blade appeared in the hedge right in front of us and Nick spun us around and we sprinted through the maze until it was all a big green blur.

I don't know how he figured out the way, but Nick had us out of the maze and halfway across the lawn before I realized we were safe, which was good because I was about to black out. I stumbled and Nick slowed, catching me before I tumbled to the ground.

"Andre, wait!" he called.

Andre turned around. His gaze went to the maze behind us, and he hurried forward to catch my other side. The two of them helped carry me up the veranda stairs where they found a stone bench for me to sit on.

"Are you all right?" Nick asked. He was checking my pulse at my wrist.

"Yeah, sure," I wheezed. "Just a little out of shape and scared witless."

"It appears we lost them," Nick said. "But we'll need to report that incident to the police." He pressed a hand to his own chest. "That was terrifying. I mean, what if they'd actually hit one of us. They could have severed . . ." He shuddered.

"Ginger! What are you doing out here?" Harry asked. "I've been looking all over for you."

"Oh, you know, the usual, running for my life," I said. He did not return my weak attempt at a smile.

Chapter 17

"What were you thinking?" Harry cried, after Nick and Andre filled him in. "I leave you alone for a few minutes and you almost get decapitated."

I put my hand to my throat. "Can we talk about something else?"

"No," he said. "Let's go find Detective Stewart, you need to tell him what happened."

"He's going to yell at me again for meddling," I said. I turned to look at Andre and Nick. "And he's going to yell at you, too."

"I just got here," Nick protested.

"He won't like that either," I said. "He's already sore that Harry is here."

"None of that matters," Harry said. "The killer is clearly

worried that you know something, and they're trying to silence you."

"I can agree to stay silent," Andre said. "Let's just make a pact not to say anything."

"And we'll, what, text the killer about our intent to not speak?" Nick asked.

"Well, it sounds ridiculous when you say it like that," Andre said.

Nick patted his shoulder. "Sorry. I didn't mean to offend, but Harrison is right. We have to speak to the detective."

Andre and I shared a pained look. This was going to be unpleasant. We entered the castle to find it was quiet. The pall over what should have been a joyous day was as heavy as a shroud. We saw Jenkins in the hallway in discussion with several of the staff. We waited to approach until he dismissed them.

"Good day, Mr. Jenkins," Harry said. "Do you know where we could find Detective Stewart?"

"He doesn't report to me," Mr. Jenkins said. His tone was tart, as if he'd been asked this question so many times he was over being polite about it.

"That's a pity," I said. "This investigation would likely be solved if you were in charge."

Mr. Jenkins straightened up, looking flattered. "Well, I have been told I have an inquisitive mind."

"I can see that," I said. "You'd have to in order to manage a place with this many moving parts. I'll bet you've been invaluable to the investigators."

Jenkins looked chuffed at my praise, which, for the

record, was sincere. Having his insight into the workings of Waverly would be an asset to the police.

"You know," he said. "Now that I think on it, I do recall that Detective Stewart was interviewing some of the staff today. If you'd like, I could tell him that you want to speak with him?"

"That would be lovely," I said.

Jenkins disappeared and we waited in the hallway. A sense of caution had me keeping an eye on every entrance in sight. After the scythe, I was fully expecting another sharp implement to come at me from any direction.

Jenkins was back in moments. He said, "Detective Stewart asked that you wait for him in the library."

"Thank you so much, Mr. Jenkins," I said. "I don't know how this place could run without you."

"Oh, I'm sure it would be fine," he said, but I could tell he was pleased.

"Well done," Harry said to me, once we were out of earshot. "You do have a way with people."

"Not really," I said. "I just see them. That's really all most people want, to be seen, acknowledged, valued. That's not asking very much, is it?"

Harry put his arm around my shoulder and pulled me against his side. "Like I said, you have a way with people."

We made our way to the library without taking any wrong turns. Once there, Andre excused himself to use the restroom, and Nick went with him to make certain nothing happened to him. We were definitely on high alert since the maze incident.

Harry and I prowled around the library. Neither of us

said it, but we were both looking for whatever Rita might have lost. I wondered if our search was in vain and Archie had already found whatever it was. Rita had sounded furious when she barked at Archie. Whatever she'd lost, it was important.

Harry took a seat in one of the wing chairs, and picked up a magazine from the table next to him. He was thumbing through the pages while I checked and rechecked the bookshelves. I was beginning to wonder if one of the books was actually a fake and when you pulled it off the shelf, it opened to a hollowed-out inside where things were hidden. Things like documents, keys, jewelry, maybe even an updated will.

Harry let out a low whistle, and I turned away from the shelf I was examining to see what the fuss was. While I watched, he turned it sideways and his eyes widened.

"What is it?" I asked.

"I think I found what Rita was looking for," he said.

I hurried across the room and glanced over his shoulder. My jaw dropped.

The photo was Rita, a younger version, but definitely Rita, wearing thigh-high red leather stiletto boots and a matching leather bustier and miniskirt, all while holding a riding crop. The expression on her face was one of invitation.

"She was a dominatrix?" I choked.

"Maybe," he said. "Perhaps she was just a model, but the outfit does look like it's out of some sort of kink catalog."

Harry flipped through the magazine. There were more

photos, and she wasn't alone in them. They removed any doubt that she was not just modeling an outfit.

"Oh, wow," Harry said.

"This is it!" I cried. "This is what she wanted Archie to find. See how the photograph was taped inside here? Someone was hiding it in plain sight."

"Pretty big risk to take," he said.

I closed the magazine to read the cover. It was a trout-fishing magazine.

"Not really," I said. "Who'd want to read this?"

He looked at me with a baleful glance.

"Other than you," I said.

"I expect it wasn't supposed to be left here on the table," he said. "Whoever had those pictures—"

"Dooney," I said. "That has to be his secret. He was blackmailing Rita with these photos. Rita, who wants nothing more than to be accepted into high society."

"Blackmailing her how?" Harry asked. "He was already marrying her daughter and giving Rita the access to society that she wanted while he was gaining a substantial chunk of their wealth."

"Yes, but the money was likely at Rita's or Matthew's discretion," I said. "With these photos, Dooney could demand whatever he wanted and they'd comply or he'd ruin them."

"I think we know who Dooney's murderer is," Harry said. "And to think the answer was sitting on this table the whole time."

"And who would that be?" Detective Stewart asked.

Harry and I whirled around to find the detective standing in the doorway to the library. Without saying a word, Harry handed the detective the magazine.

Detective Stewart frowned at the cover. "Trout fishing?"

"Page sixty," I said.

"And seventy, and so on," Harry added.

The detective flipped open the magazine. His eyebrows shot up. He flipped through some more pages and then slammed the magazine shut.

"Where did you find this?"

"Here on the coffee table while we were waiting for you," Harry said.

Detective Stewart nodded. "A moment, please."

He turned and strode to the door. A constable was there, and they had a whispered conversation.

"Horrible thought," I said to Harry. "You don't reckon he thinks we planted this, do you?"

"No, that'd be daft," Harry said.

Detective Stewart came back. "Convenient for you to have just stumbled upon this, don't you think?"

"Daft, did you say?" I muttered to Harry. He gave me a quelling look.

"I wouldn't say it was convenient so much as dumb luck, and you're the one to thank," Harry said.

"How do you figure?"

"If you hadn't asked us to wait in the library, we wouldn't have been in here," Harry said. "So, in many ways, you're the one who found the photos, don't you think?"

Detective Stewart seemed to like that take on things. I beamed at Harry. My talent of people pleasing was certainly wearing off on him, although in this case, he was stretching the truth.

"Excuse me, you wanted to see me, Detective?" Rita May entered the room. She looked as elegant as ever. She definitely had the Audrey Hepburn, timeless beauty thing happening. Reconciling this woman with the vixen in the photos made my brain hurt.

Piper followed her mother into the room and asked, "Will this take long? I need my mother with me, today of all days."

I reached over and grabbed Harry's hand. Did Piper know? I doubted it. She was the privileged daughter of wealthy parents who had protected her from everything. I imagined that "everything" included her mother's unsavory past.

The detective cleared his throat. "It'll take just a moment. A private word over here, perhaps, Mrs. May?"

Rita nodded and followed him to the other side of the room. He showed her the cover of the magazine and she looked bored. He opened it up and she went pale and stumbled back a few steps, shaking her head as if she could deny what she was seeing, and then she fainted. She landed on the floor so hard that if she hadn't already blacked out, she'd have knocked herself out for certain.

"Mum!" Piper cried. She hurried to her mother's side and crouched down.

Detective Stewart looked at me and Harry and yelled, "Get help!"

"Stay here," Harry ordered and he ran from the room.

That was an easy order to follow as I stood there frozen, not knowing what to do.

"Mrs. May, are you all right?" Detective Stewart was kneeling on the other side of Rita. He was checking the pulse at her wrist and frowning in concern.

Her eyelids fluttered and she stared up at him. "I know how awful it looks, but I didn't do it."

"Do what?" Piper asked. "You need to see a doctor."

"No, I'm fine," Rita insisted.

"Can you sit up?" Detective Stewart asked.

She nodded, then took his hand and let him help her to a nearby chair.

"Were the . . . uh . . . photos what you asked Archie Carlton to find for you?"

"How do you know about that?" Rita's pale face flamed red. "Did he tell you that?"

"It doesn't matter how I know," Detective Stewart said. "The fact is that it gives you a real motive to have murdered Dooney Portis."

"What?" Piper cried. "Are you out of your mind? My mother would never." She turned to Rita. "What is he talking about, Mum? What photos?"

Rita exhaled as if she knew the battle was lost. This was it, I thought, she was going to confess.

"When I was very young, I did some modeling," Rita said. "The poses were risqué."

Detective Stewart and I said nothing, which I thought was very good of us given that "risqué" was quite the understatement, even by British standards.

"I don't understand," Piper said. "What does that have to do with Dooney?"

"He was blackmailing me," Rita said.

She was the woman we heard in the garden on the day we arrived. It had to have been her, yelling at Dooney about ruining her. It all clicked. Dooney was blackmailing Rita with those photos, so she'd murdered him.

Piper blinked. She looked confused. "I don't understand. Why would Dooney blackmail you?"

"Because marrying into money wasn't enough for him," Rita said. "He wanted more and more and more."

"So, you killed him," Detective Stewart said.

"No, I didn't," Rita protested. "I would never. Yes, I wanted the blackmail to stop but I would never have murdered him. I paid him but he refused to give me the photos."

"What about your husband?" Detective Stewart asked. "Did Dooney go to your husband?"

"No." Rita looked sick. "He doesn't know about the blackmail or the photos. Please don't tell him. He'd never forgive me for—"

"For what? Murder? I suppose Quentin blackmailed you, too, so you murdered him as well. You're a monster." Piper recoiled.

"Piper, darling, no!" Rita sobbed. "I didn't murder Dooney. I would never have murdered him, knowing how much you loved him. And, no, Quentin wasn't blackmailing me. Only Dooney. You have to believe me."

"Well, I don't!" Piper said. "Quentin was Dooney's best friend and Dooney told him everything. Clearly,

Quentin knew about those photos, and when Dooney died, he took over blackmailing you, didn't he?"

"No!" Rita insisted. She looked desperate, and I couldn't tell if she was lying or not.

"We're going to have to take you in for formal questioning," Detective Stewart said. I noticed he was still holding the fishing magazine.

"I want my husband," Rita said.

"We can collect him on the way," he said. He looked at Piper and me. "Kindly wait here. I'll send a colleague to interview you both shortly."

"Piper, please." Rita made one last attempt to get Piper to listen to her, but her daughter wasn't having it.

"I hope you rot in prison, Mum," Piper said. "I can't believe you murdered the man I love."

"I didn't," Rita said. "I swear I didn't."

The silence that filled the room after she left felt needle sharp and I was afraid to say anything, as if it could prick my skin and make me bleed. I had no idea how to ease the tension.

"This is a nightmare," Piper said. She sank onto one of the upholstered chairs.

Not knowing what to do while we waited, I sat down, too.

"I'm sorry," I said. This felt woefully inadequate. "It must be a horrible shock."

Piper glanced at the grandfather clock in the corner. Her face was a mask of misery. "I should be getting married right now."

I said nothing. What could I say? Her groom was dead.

Her mother had murdered him. Piper was right—it was a nightmare.

"I was going to be a beautiful bride," she said. She glanced at me with a sad expression. "And my bridesmaids would have looked so lovely in those hats of Viv's. They are so much prettier than the ones Javier made."

"I thought Javier fled the country without making the hats," I said. "Isn't that why you wanted Viv?"

"Of course," Piper said. "What I meant was that Viv's hats were much nicer than the sketches Javier showed me."

I nodded. I thought about Javier, supposedly fleeing the country after poisoning his lover. Suddenly the story felt weird. Off. Too convenient.

"Dooney and I were going to be so happy," Piper said. She touched the corners of her eyes with the back of her hand as if to stop the flow of tears. Except her eyes didn't look watery at all.

Sunny said she'd been having an affair with Dooney, and I believed her. Could Piper really just put that aside? It seemed improbable to me. I mean, the man was having a child with another woman, assuming, of course, that Sunny was telling the truth about the baby being Dooney's and that they'd been in love. At the moment, I was doubtful of everyone and everything.

"You didn't know about your mother's . . . um . . . modeling past?" I asked.

Piper shook her head. "No, and at the moment, I don't feel as if I ever really knew her at all. She murdered Dooney and then Quentin just to keep some smutty pictures of herself in red leather, brandishing a riding crop from becoming public. What sort of psychopath does that?"

She was twirling a long lock of hair around her finger, studying the ends. She was the picture of innocence. But her words belied the pose.

My heart thumped hard in my chest. The detective hadn't shown Piper the photos in the magazine and Piper said she didn't know about her mother's past. But Piper had just revealed that she *had* seen the pictures before by describing them perfectly. Why lie? I could think of only one reason.

My thoughts must have shown on my face because Piper studied me and then licked her lips and said, "At least, I assume that's what the pictures look like. Did you see them?"

I glanced at the door. Where was the constable? For that matter, where was Harry with help? What had happened to everyone? I needed someone to come in here right now because by Piper's own admission, she'd known about the pictures, and I suspected she was in on the blackmail scheme, too. In fact, in that moment, I was willing to bet she'd engineered the whole thing.

"You murdered Dooney, didn't you?" I asked.

She dropped her hand and smoothed her skirt, taking a long pause before she glanced up at me. "I don't know what you're talking about."

"You found out about Sunny and the baby and Dooney's plan to leave you for her after he cashed out on the blackmail, so you killed him," I said.

"You're mistaken," Piper said. "There's no proof that Sunny's baby is Dooney's. He loved me."

"Did he?" I asked. "Or did he love her and when you found out about it, you decided to murder him and have Sunny take the fall? That's why she was in your wedding party, wasn't it? You needed her here so you could make it appear like she poisoned him because he wouldn't leave you for her, when it was actually the opposite."

"Does Harrison enjoy these flights of fancy of yours?" Piper asked. "I think they're tiresome."

I ignored her. My head was spinning with all of the implications of her actions.

"The blackmail was your idea all along," I said. "I'm assuming because your parents were not giving you everything you wanted for the wedding. Your father mentioned something about the cost of hats. He didn't seem pleased."

"He's as cheap as chips and not in a good way," she said. Her expression was pinched in displeasure. "But that doesn't mean I had anything to do with Dooney blackmailing my mum."

"Except you knew exactly what she was wearing in the photos, so you've obviously seen them," I said.

She feigned a yawn as if I was boring her.

"What I can't figure out is why you murdered Quentin," I said.

"Because I didn't?"

"You said Dooney told him everything and you accused your mother of murdering Quentin because he took over blackmailing her," I said. I shook my head. "But he didn't have the photos, so I'm guessing he wasn't blackmailing her, was he?" She stared at me with a death glare that, I'm not going to lie, was very intimidating. Still, I continued. "He was blackmailing you."

"That's ridiculous," Piper scoffed. "What could he possibly blackmail me for?"

It was a shot in the dark, but I went for it. "For being the person who cooked up the blackmail scheme to begin with? Quentin was going to go to your parents, wasn't he?"

She continued to stare daggers at me and my heart rate picked up. Where was the constable? Still, it was thrilling to have my powers of deduction firing on all engines. I wished Harry were here to see me busting the case wide open. Where was he? For that matter, where were Andre and Nick?

"Was it Quentin going to your parents and telling them it was you who'd planned the blackmail that made you decide to murder him, or was it the amount of money he was asking for?" I asked.

She laughed but it was a bitter sound. "He didn't want money. He wanted me. He thought I'd marry him to keep things quiet. Ha! You do realize you can't prove any of this. It's all just speculation."

"Can't I?" I asked. "The one thing that Dooney and Quentin had in common was that they both drank very expensive Macallan whiskey right before they died. Is that where you put the poison, in the bottle of whiskey?"

Her lips puckered and her eyes narrowed. "You think you're so clever, don't you, party crasher?" she asked. "Well, you're not. I'm smarter and prettier and more powerful than you'll ever be, and when you're dead, who do you think is going to console your heartbroken fiancé?"

Her smile was pure evil. She wrinkled her nose and said, "Not to ruin the ending for you, but it'll be me."

I scoffed. "Harry would never have you." My voice came out strong and I was grateful because, quite frankly, she was scaring the snot out of me. "It was you in the maze, wasn't it? You're the one who tried to kill me with the scythe."

She shrugged. "Not kill you so much as permanently disfigure you. I was hoping to slice off your face so Harry would dump you."

I swallowed hard. Okay, I was downshifting from impressed with myself to scared to absolutely terrified. I glanced at the door again. She followed the line of my gaze. Then she rose from her seat and crossed the room to close the door. She turned the old skeleton key in the lock and tossed it across the room. I was locked in with her.

"You're right," she said. "Someone will be here soon. I'd best dispatch you before that happens. It's cold comfort, I know, but you can die knowing how very clever you are."

I knew I could run and she would chase me or I could plow right into her and, hopefully, catch her off guard. I chose the latter, thinking it was the less obvious choice. With a yell, I launched myself at her.

Chapter 18

I did catch her off guard. Yay, me. But as we hit the ground, she clobbered me with a vicious backhand that I did not see coming and it threw me across the floor.

It took me a beat to get my bearings. I pushed up onto my hands and knees. My face stung where she'd struck me, which just made me mad.

"How exactly are you planning to explain my murder?" I asked. "Don't you think the police will find it highly suspicious that I was left alone with you and then I was suddenly dead when they came back?"

She reached into her pocket and pulled out a very long, very lethal-looking knife. "You were consumed with jealousy that I had dated your fiancé before you. You came at me with a knife that you must have taken from the kitchen. We fought and while I was defending myself, I stabbed you. Such a tragedy."

"No one is going to believe that," I said.

"They will," she said. "Daddy will make sure of it. Just like he bought those photographs from the man who tried to blackmail him with them so many years ago."

"You mean your father knows about the pictures?" I asked.

"Of course," she said. "I found them in his office safe. My mother didn't know that he had them, obviously, or we never would have been able to blackmail her."

"Don't you think your father is going to figure out that you're the one who took the photos and gave them to Dooney to torture your mother with?" I asked.

"No," she said. But there was a glimmer of doubt in her voice.

She blinked at me and I remembered something I'd read about criminals not being very smart, which was why they usually got caught. Piper was going to get caught. I had no doubt about that. I just wanted to live long enough to see her go to jail. There was only one way out of this room, and I really hoped she didn't know about it.

I rose to my feet. She crouched low, gripping the knife in her right hand with the blade tilted up. She looked like she knew what she was doing. I wondered if she'd ever stabbed anyone before, and I wouldn't have been surprised to hear the answer was yes.

Judging the distance between us, she could charge me and stab me and I'd be bleeding out before I could stop her. I didn't like the balance of power in the room. I moved closer to a stack of books.

"Stop moving!" she demanded.

"I'm sorry," I said. "Did you expect me to stand still while you stab me?" As I asked the question, I grabbed a book and threw it at her. She raised her hands to defend herself and managed to stab the book. It got stuck on the knife, rendering it useless. I threw three more books at her, knocking her to her knees while she struggled to pull the knife free.

I took advantage of the opportunity and ran to the door that led to the tunnel. Thankfully, it wasn't locked. I yanked it open and ran down the steps, not bothering to turn the light on. It was cold and dank and dark, but I felt safer in the shadows than I would have if the light were on.

The door opened behind me, and I could hear Piper swearing as she navigated the steps. It remained dark, so she obviously didn't know about the light switches. I decided to use the cover of darkness. She couldn't see me. She didn't know where I was. I moved swiftly but quietly on the stone path, hoping to reach the end before she could pinpoint my location and stab me.

"I know you're down here," Piper cried. "This only makes my plan even stronger. You forced me down here at knifepoint. It was dark. In the tussle, I stabbed you. It's perfect."

My stomach roiled. I had no doubt she would stab me and let me bleed out if she could. She'd murdered twice. What was one more person? I picked up my pace as quietly as I could.

I used my fingers to guide my path along the wall. I had to be about halfway through now. Just be quiet for a little bit farther, I told myself, but my curiosity wasn't having it.

"Did Javier give you the same cyanide he used on his lover to put in Dooney's whiskey?" I asked.

Her laugh was low and sinister and much closer than I liked. "Why do you care?"

Ha! She didn't deny it. That was it. That was how she'd managed to kill both Dooney and Quentin. She'd definitely poisoned their drinks!

"Because when I get out of here, I'm telling Detective Stewart," I said.

"You're not getting out of here," she scoffed. "In fact, I have to thank you for accessing this tunnel. This is so much more dramatic than my original plan. I'll be able to stage the death scene for premium optics."

Great, she'd pivoted from mourning her wedding day to planning my death day without breaking a sweat. Well, not today, Piper. Even though it meant I might lose my balance, I let go of the wall. I had to get to the door at the end of the tunnel with enough time to open it before she finished me off. Death, the great motivator. I began to sprint. To heck with the type of poison. I had to get out of here.

The footsteps behind me picked up speed, but I had the advantage. I'd been in here before. I ran through a pocket of cold air and shivered. That was weird. It made me slow down, and instead of slamming into the door, I stumbled into it. I felt around for the handle and grabbed it. It turned and I pushed but it didn't budge. Oh, no. It was stuck. Piper was going to catch me and stab me to death and no one would ever know the truth—that Piper May was the real killer.

I pushed and slapped the wood and cursed under my breath. It didn't budge and Piper was closing in fast. I could hear her panting behind me. I wanted to cry but I didn't have the energy. I braced myself against the door and suddenly it gave way.

Falling backward out of the tunnel, I blinked against the late-afternoon light, which seemed very bright given my last few minutes spent in the dark. A pair of strong arms caught me, and I glanced up. Harrison!

"Piper is right behind me," I gasped. "She has a knife. She's the real killer."

"Detective!" Harry bellowed as he dragged me away from the open door.

Stewart and a constable jogged up to us right as Piper was stepping out of the tunnel. She held the knife in one hand and was blinking against the daylight. As soon as she locked in on the detective, she cried, "Arrest that woman, she tried to kill me!"

I scoffed. "Right. Who's holding the knife, Piper?"

"Calm down, ladies," Detective Stewart said. "Just calm down."

"Don't you dare tell me to calm down," Piper cried. She pointed the knife at the detective, who wisely backed up.

I certainly didn't agree with Piper on, well, anything, but even I had to admit it is very patronizing when a man

255

tells you to calm down, especially when you have every right to be upset. And I did have a right to be upset because I'd almost been killed.

"Ms. May, put the knife down," Detective Stewart said. His tone didn't allow for negotiation but Piper didn't seem to care.

"No." She pointed the knife in my direction. "She'll kill me if I don't protect myself."

"With the detective standing right here?" I asked. "Does that seem even remotely likely?"

"You are unstable," she said. "You crashed the party of your boyfriend and threw cake at him in a jealous rage. Of course you will kill me for being the love of your fiancé's life."

"What?" Harry cried. "We went on two dates. Two terrible dates."

"It's all right, Harrison," she said. "I love you, too."

Okay, now she was pushing my buttons. She stepped away from the tunnel, still brandishing the knife. I glanced past her and there was Viv, lurking in the shadows of the doorway. She put her finger to her lips.

"Don't talk to my fiancé like that," I said. I tried to look jealous or furious, hoping to distract Piper from noticing any movement behind her.

"I'll talk to him any way I like," Piper said. "You don't actually think he's going to marry you now that I'm available again, do you?"

Detective Stewart's eyes went wide. In her play to make me jealous, she'd also outed herself as not caring that the man she should have been marrying right that very moment was dead.

"Ms. May, that seems very coldhearted of you, and on your wedding day," Detective Stewart said. His eyes narrowed in suspicion.

Piper immediately struck a dramatic pose, putting the back of her hand on her forehead. "Goodness, I don't know what I'm saying. Wrestling the knife from her when she tried to kill me has made me quite distraught."

I rolled my eyes. "That did not happen."

Piper opened her mouth to argue, and it was the moment Viv needed. She launched herself out of the tunnel and grabbed Piper about the knees, taking her down with a solid thump. Piper dropped the knife and started to wheeze.

With the wind knocked out of her, Piper was helpless. It gave the detective and constable the opportunity to put her in restraints. The detective picked up the knife by the blade and dropped it into his pocket. Then he and the constable dragged Piper to her feet.

She struggled against their hold, while Harry and I hurried to help Viv up.

"Are you all right?" I asked. I took one arm while Harry took the other.

"Right as rain," Viv said. We lifted her to a standing position. "And you?"

"I'm fine," I said. "Thankfully the tunnel was an escape route. I almost lost it when the door was stuck but Harry opened it just in time."

"Yeah, someone moved a large boulder in front of it," Harry said. He frowned at the detective.

"We were trying to keep people from accessing the castle through it." He gestured to a very large rock at the side of the door. "Hardly a boulder."

"I ran into Harrison when I was walking Dominick out. Harrison was waiting for the ambulance and told me where you were," said Viv. "I had three heart attacks when I arrived at the library and the door was locked and no one was answering. Luckily, it was an easy lock to open."

"A family talent?" Harry asked me. I shrugged.

"When I got the door open and you weren't in there, I knew something was wrong. Then I saw that the door in the back of the room was open to that creepy passageway," Viv said. She turned to Stewart. "I heard everything that was said in the tunnel. Piper murdered both Dooney and Quentin. She poisoned their drinks."

Detective Stewart's eyebrows went up. "Are you certain? The medical examiner speculated poison killed them but said the toxicology report wouldn't be in for a few more days."

"Tell him to look for cyanide," I said. "Piper's former hat designer, Javier Sebastian, was accused of murdering his lover with cyanide and I believe he's the one who gave the poison to Piper."

"Piper was going to kill Scarlett to keep her quiet," Viv concluded.

Harry slid his arm around my waist and pulled me

close. "I step away for one minute and you solve the murders and almost get yourself killed," he muttered.

I patted his chest, trying to comfort him.

"How did you figure it out?" Detective Stewart asked me.

"That the drinks were poisoned?" I clarified. "I remembered that Javier had fled the country after poisoning his lover and that Piper had met him at a fashion show before that. It seemed only logical that Piper decided to use the same method to get rid of Dooney. Both men had been drinking expensive whiskey right before they died, so I suspected she poisoned the bottle and used it on both of them. In fact, I'll bet Quentin's glass will still have trace amounts of the poison. If you kept everything from the crime scene, that would put a lock on it."

I turned to Piper. "You told me the day I met you that you chose Javier as your milliner because you'd recently met him at India Couture Week. If I remember right, India is one of the few places you can still purchase cyanide."

"If you bribe the right people. Isn't that so, Piper?" Viv asked.

"You're being ridiculous," Piper protested. "So what if I was in India at the same time as Javier? You can't prove anything."

"No, but he can," Viv said. She nodded at Detective Stewart and his chest swelled.

"After you left the room with Rita, Piper described the . . . er . . . outfit Rita was wearing in the photographs," I began. "But she had just said she knew nothing about the photographs. I guessed that she was the one who gave the photos to Dooney to blackmail Rita. Dooney, of course, told Quentin all about Piper's scheme. Then Quentin tried to blackmail Piper after Dooney died. Unless she agreed to marry him, he would tell her parents that she was the one who thought up the blackmail scheme to get more money out of them for her wedding. Knowing this would cause her parents to cut her off from the family money, she decided to kill him and set up her mother as the murderer instead."

"Lies, lies, lies," Piper said. "It's all lies. You're going to look bloody stupid if you listen to this twaddle and arrest me. My mother is the killer and Scarlett tried to kill me because her fiancé is still in love with me."

Harry cringed and shook his head. "No. Absolutely unequivocally no."

"Yeah, I didn't think so either," Detective Stewart said. "Come along, Ms. May. Let's go see what your parents have to say about all of this."

We watched them walk away and Viv stepped up and hugged me. "I'm so glad you're all right."

"Me, too," I said. "Your timing was brilliant."

"Good thing I walked Dominick out and ran into Harrison," she said.

"Very good thing," Harry agreed.

The three of us began to walk back to the castle. I noticed none of us wanted to use the tunnel. Even with the light on, if I never went in there again, it was just fine with me.

Back inside the castle, we found Andre and Nick waiting for us in the suite with Fee and Alistair and Bella, who was so happy to see Harry and me that she lost all sense of doggy decorum. I was right there with her. The sight of her pointy ears and stubby legs made my heart feel so full it actually hurt. I had missed my baby girl something fierce.

I dropped to the floor and gave her all the belly rubs she required. Once she calmed down, I glanced up at my friends.

"Where were you?" I asked Andre and Nick. "You were supposed to come back to the library."

They exchanged a sheepish glance.

"Sorry," Andre said. "We got distracted by the art. Have you seen the portraits in this place?"

"They're delightfully snooty," Nick added. "Absolutely dripping with disdain."

Having had the same thought myself, I couldn't fault them. I gave them an exasperated look and said, "Okay, I get it."

"And what are you doing here?" Harry asked after Alistair had swooped down on Viv and given her a proper kiss hello.

"Fee and I were feeling horribly left out," Alistair said.

"Utterly," Fee agreed.

"And I wanted to check on Sunny and make certain that my colleague was able to take her case," Alistair continued. "I'm pleased to say he was, but now it won't be necessary. He just texted me that she's been released and is going home to her mum's house in Devon."

"Oh, wonderful," I said. I made a mental note to reach

out to her. I expected that being a single mother was going to be a challenge.

"We decided we'd come and collect you all, not knowing that my girl would be the one to take the villain down," Alistair said. "Very brave of you, love, but please don't ever do that again."

"It was Scarlett's fault," Viv said.

"Hey!" I protested.

"It was," Viv said. "You're the one who wanted to take this job so that you could examine the castle and see if it suited you for a wedding venue."

"She's right, your obsession with your wedding got us into this mess," Andre agreed. "Now I *propose* we get out of here."

I rolled my eyes.

"Onto our next *engagement*?" Alistair asked.

"Make them stop," I muttered to Harry. He grinned down at me.

"We can be on our *marry* way as soon as I pack," Viv said.

I gritted my teeth.

"I *vow* this has been an exciting day, yeah," Fee said. I glowered and she laughed.

I glanced at Nick and Harry. "Go ahead, get it out before you explode."

"Scarlett, dearest." Nick put his hand on his chest. "We were just *groomed* to be punny."

"Even if our *reception* is not always what we'd wish," Harry said.

They all laughed, but I shook my head.

"Those were all terrible," I said. "Truly, even a wedding cake would be in *tiers* over those." No one laughed. They didn't even groan. "Oh, come on," I cried. "Wedding cake? Tiers? That was funny."

No one chuckled. Not even a snicker. Although Harry did smile.

"All right, Ginger, let's go pack," Harry said. He took me by the hand and led me out the door.

I didn't turn around but called over my shoulder, "I see you all trying not to laugh." Much to my satisfaction, as the door closed after us, I did hear someone snort. I knew they thought my puns were funny. Ha!

While we were packing, I paused by the window, taking one last long look at the beautiful castle and the rolling green hills.

"Harry, remember how we agreed that we didn't care about the ceremony so long as we were married at the end of it?"

"Yes," he said. He was rolling his clothes into his carry-on bag.

"Then I have an idea," I said.

He stopped packing and looked at me. "I'm listening."

"Let's elope." I clasped my hands in front of my chest. Of the two of us, Harry was the less impulsive, more traditional one. If he didn't want to do this, that was fine, but it just felt right and I was hoping he felt the same way, because, truly, after the madness of this weekend, I just wanted a small wedding with our nearest and dearest and the sooner the better.

His smile was slow and sure. "When do we leave?"

Acknowledgments

Thank you to everyone who loves the Hat Shop Mysteries and much gratitude to my publisher, who invites me to write them as time allows.

Special thanks to Christina Hogrebe, Kate Seaver and Amanda Maurer for keeping me on task and supporting all the ideas that demand to be written.

Much gratitude to the amazing art department, and cover artist Robert Gantt Steele and book designer Laura K. Corless. You capture the spirit of the books perfectly.

Shout-out to the team at Berkley who supports me in a million ways I don't even know about, particularly Jessica Mangicaro and Dache' Rogers. I appreciate your enthusiasm so much!

Keep reading for an excerpt from
Jenn McKinlay's new rom-com

SUMMER READING

The ferry from Woods Hole to Martha's Vineyard was standing room only. Shoulder to shoulder, hip to hip, the passengers were packed as tight as two coats of paint. I had a rowdy group of college kids at my back, which was fine as I'd carved out a spot at the rail near the bow of the ship and was taking in big gulps of salty sea air while counting down the seconds of the forty-five-minute ride.

It was the first time in ten years I'd returned to the Gale family cottage in Oak Bluffs for an extended stay—I'd only managed quick weekends here and there around my busy work schedule—and I was feeling mostly anxious with a flicker of anticipation. Preoccupied with the idea of spending the entire summer on island, I did not hear the commotion at my back until it was almost too late.

"Bruh!" a deep voice yelled.

I turned around to see a gaggle of man-boys in matching T-shirts—it took my neurodivergent brain a moment to decipher the Greek letters on their shirts, identifying them as frat boys—roughhousing behind me.

Is "gaggle" the right word? I'm sure they'd have preferred something cool like "squad" but, honestly, with their baggy shorts, sideways ball caps and sparsely whiskered chins, they looked more like a cackle of hyenas or a pandemonium of parrots. Either way, one of them was noticeably turning a sickly shade of green, and his cheeks started to swell. When he began to convulse as if a demon was punching its way up from his stomach, his friends scrambled to get away from him.

I realized with horror that he was going to vomit and the only thing between him and the open sea was me, trapped against the railing. In a panic, I looked for a viable exit. Unfortunately, I was penned in by a stalwart woman with headphones on and a hot guy reading a book. I had a split second to decide who would be easier to move. I went with Reader Guy, simply because I figured he could at least hear me when I yelled, "Move!"

I was wrong. He didn't hear me and he didn't move. In fact, he was so nonresponsive it was like he was on another planet. As the dude doing the herky-jerky lunged toward me, I gave the man a nudge. He didn't respond. Desperate, I slapped my hand over the words in his book.

He snapped his head in my direction with a peeved expression. Then he looked past me and his eyes went wide. In one motion, he grabbed me and pulled me down and to the side, out of the line of fire.

The puker almost made it to the rail. Almost. I heard the hot splat of vomit on the deck behind me and hoped it didn't land on the backs of my shoes. Mercifully, Reader Guy's quick thinking shielded me from the worst of it. Frat Boy was hanging over the railing and, as the vomiting started in earnest, the crowd finally pressed back, way back, and we scuttled out of the blast zone.

My rescuer let go of me and asked, "Are you all right?"

I opened my mouth to answer when the smell hit me. That distinctive stomach-churning, nose-wrinkling, gag-inducing smell that accompanies undigested food and bile. My mouth pooled with saliva and I felt my throat convulse. This was an emergency of epic proportions as I am a sympathy puker. You puke, I puke, we all puke. Truly, if someone hurls near me, it becomes a gastro-geyser of Old Faithful proportions. I spun away from the man in a flurry of arms that slapped his book out of his hands and sent it careening toward the ocean.

He let out a yell and made a grab for it. He missed and leaned over the railing, looking as if he was actually contemplating making a dive for it.

I felt terrible and would have apologized, but I was too busy holding my fist to my mouth while trying not to lose my breakfast. The egg-and-bacon sandwich I'd enjoyed suddenly seemed like the worst decision ever and it took all of my powers of concentration not to hurl. I tried to breathe through my mouth but the retching sounds Frat Boy was making were not helping.

"Come on." Reader Guy took my arm and helped me move farther away. I turned my head in case I was sick. I could feel my stomach heaving and then—

"*Ouch!* You pinched me!" I cried.

My hero—although that seemed like an overstatement given that he had just inflicted pain upon my person—had nipped the skin on the inside of my elbow with enough force to startle me and make me rub my arm.

"Still feel like throwing up?" he asked.

I paused to assess my stomach situation. The episode had passed. I blinked at him. He was taller than me. Lean with broad shoulders and wavy dark brown hair that reached his shoulders. He had nice features, arching eyebrows, sculpted cheekbones, and a defined jaw covered in a thin layer of scruff. His eyes were a blue-gray much like the ocean surrounding us. Dressed in a navy sweatshirt, khaki shorts and black lace-up work boots, he looked like a local.

He stared at me expectantly, and I realized he'd asked a question and was waiting for an answer. Feeling like an idiot for blatantly checking him out, I attempted to play it off as if I was still wrestling with the urge to upchuck. I raised my hand in a *wait* gesture and then slowly nodded.

"No, I think I'm okay," I said. "Thank you."

"You're welcome," he said. Then he smiled at me—it was a dazzler—making me forget the horror of the last few minutes. "You tossed my book into the ocean."

"I'm so sorry," I said. Nervousness and relief that I

hadn't lost my breakfast caused me to try to make light of the situation. This was a bad play. "At least it was just a book and not an essential item, but I'll absolutely buy you a replacement."

"Not necessary." He frowned at me and looked at where the paperback was now polluting the ocean—one more thing for me to feel bad about—and then back at me and said, "I take it you're not a reader."

And there it was, the judgmental tone I'd heard my whole life when it became known that I was not a natural-born reader. Why were book people always so perplexed by non–book people? I mean, it's not like I wanted to be dyslexic. As usual when I'm feeling defensive about my disability, I said the most offensive thing I could think of.

"Books are boring," I responded. Yes, I, Samantha Gale, went there. I knew full well this was likely heresy for this guy, and I was right. His reaction did not disappoint.

His mouth dropped open. His eyes went wide. He blinked. "Don't hold back. Say what you feel."

"Why would I read a book when I can just stream the movie version, which allows me to use both hands to cram popcorn into my face at the same time?" I asked.

"Because the book is *always* better than the movie."

I shook my head. "I disagree. There's no way the book version of *Jaws* was better than the movie."

"Ah!" he yelped. If he'd been wearing pearls, I was sure he'd be clutching them.

When he was about to argue, I cut him off with the *duuun-dun duuun-dun duuun-dun dun dun dun* sound from the iconic *Jaws* theme music.

Reader Guy laughed and raised his hands in defeat. "Did you pick that movie because we're on our way to the location where it was filmed?"

I shrugged. "Maybe. Also, it was the first movie that popped into my head."

"I wonder if sharks are big readers?" he asked. He peered down at the water. His book had soaked up enough of the sea that it was slowly dropping beneath the surface, sinking down to Davy Jones's locker forevermore. I glanced back at his face. He looked as if he was in actual physical pain.

"You all right?" I asked.

"Not really," he said. He rubbed his knuckles over his chest as if his heart hurt. "I was just getting to the good part."

I had to force myself not to roll my eyes. It was just a book. I thought about abandoning Reader Guy to his grief, but it seemed impolite since he *had* saved me from a fountain of barf and I *had* accidentally smacked his book into the drink, and besides he *was* cute in a buy-local sort of way.

"I really am sorry," I said. "Was it a rare book or super valuable?" I hoped not. Being in between chef jobs was not leaving my bank account flush.

"No, it was just the latest Joe Pickett mystery from C. J. Box." He shrugged. "I'm just stuck at a cliffhanger without it."

"Oh, that is a bummer." Personally, I hated cliffhangers on my shows—*Just give her the rose already!*—so I imagined the feeling wasn't any better with a book. I glanced at the choppy water below as if I could manifest the book and make it rise out of the ocean and float back to the boat in perfect condition. See? Just because I don't read, that doesn't mean I don't have an imagination.

"It's fine, really," he said.

One thing I'd learned in my twenty-eight circles around the sun was that when a person said it was fine, it never ever was. I glanced up and noticed we were approaching the pier.

"Listen, I'm happy to replace it, really," I said. I reached into my shoulder bag, wondering how much cash I had in my wallet. My nausea threatened to punch back at the thought of how broke I was.

He put his hand over mine, stopping me. His skin was warm despite the cool breeze blowing in from the water. He gave my fingers a quick squeeze before he let go and said, "It really is okay. Accidents happen."

We'd leveled up to "okay." Well, all right then. "Okay" usually did mean exactly that. I smiled at him, relieved. His gaze met mine and for a second I forgot about everything—my anxiety about returning to Oak Bluffs after so long, the nature of my responsibilities while on island this summer, the low balance in my checking account, the future of my culinary career—and suddenly it was very important to me that this guy not think badly of me. Why? I had no idea, it just was.

"You know, it's not so much that I'm not a reader as my occupation keeps me too busy to find time," I said. "There's not a lot of downtime to curl up with a novel in my world."

The wind whipped my long black hair across my face as if to chastise me for being a fibber. Whatever. I hooked my finger around the hank of hair and pulled it away from my mouth.

Reader Guy leaned an elbow on the railing. Now I had his attention. "When you do have time, what do you like to read?"

Uh-oh. I hadn't really thought the natural conversational trajectory through. Shit. I scanned my brain for the title of a book—*any* book.

"Stephen King," I said. One does not grow up in New England and not know the King. "Big fan. Huge." Not a lie, because I'd watched all of the movies repeatedly.

"So you like the scary stuff?" he asked. "Like Stephen Graham Jones, Riley Sager and Simone St. James?"

The heat of the sun beat down on my head. Why was it suddenly so hot out here? Who was I kidding? This guy was book smart and I was a book moron. Why was I even trying to converse with him?

"Yup, all those guys. Horror's my jam," I agreed. Before he could ask me any more questions, I spun it around. "How about you? Who are your go-to authors?"

He looked thoughtful and said, "Oh, you know, Kafka, Joyce, Proust . . ."

Even I, the nonreader, knew those were literary heavy hitters. My voice came out a little higher than normal when I asked, "For fun?"

His blue-gray eyes met mine, and I saw a spark of mischief in them. Relieved, I burst out laughing and swatted his forearm. "Funny, really funny."

His return grin was like getting hit by a blast of sunshine at the end of a long winter. "What gave it away?"

"Joyce is not really known for his cliffhangers," I said. I hadn't read any of that stuff since my D-minus attempt at Eng 101, but I still remembered there were no creepy cornfields to be found in James Joyce. Pity.

He snapped his fingers. "Should have gone with Shakespeare."

A gentle bump indicated that we'd landed, and as the boat rocked beneath our feet, he reached out a hand to steady me. A current of awareness rippled through me and I was about to ask his name when a shout brought my attention back in the direction of the puker.

"Hey, miss!" I turned and saw one of the frat bros had my duffel bag by the handle. "Is this yours?"

It was! I had completely forgotten it. I took a few steps toward the guy when I remembered my new friend. I turned back but the crowd was already filling the space between us.

I called out to Reader Guy, "Sorry, I have to—"

A large family shuffled into the gap, cutting off my words as everyone scrambled for the exit while avoiding the vomit-contaminated area. I was jostled right into the young man with my bag, and when I glanced back, all I could see of my new friend was the top of his head. He raised his hand and waved over the crowd. I returned the gesture, feeling very unsatisfied by our parting. I hadn't gotten his name or anything, which did not stop me from hoping I'd run into him again.

Martha's Vineyard was less than one hundred square miles. Surely I'd see him at some point. Right?